HEARTS COLLIDE

Ann Patrick

A KISMET™ Romance

METEOR PUBLISHING CORPORATION
Bensalem, Pennsylvania

KISMET™ is a trademark of Meteor Publishing Corporation

Copyright © 1991 Patricia A. Kay
Cover Art Copyright © 1991 Jack Martin

First Printing April 1991.

ISBN: 1-878702-37-8

Printed in the United States of America

This book is dedicated to all the wonderful, supportive members of the Romance Writers of America, but most especially to Emma Merritt. You are the best!

ANN PATRICK

Ann Patrick was the kind of kid who always had her nose stuck in a book. For years she dreamed about being a writer. Finally, when her three children were grown, she decided to do something about her life-long wish and has been writing ever since. "I love writing," she says. "There's no greater thrill in the world than having someone say they like what you've written." Ann and her husband, along with their two cats, live in Houston, Texas.

ONE

Paula Romano knew she was in trouble. Only minutes ago she'd been driving along Richmond Avenue, minding her own business, enjoying the balmy October day so typical of Houston while she sang along with a Billy Joel tape. Now here she was, standing in shards of glass, face-to-face with a furious man. A gorgeous, furious man, she amended.

"Are you crazy?" he shouted as he stalked toward her. "Why did you hit your brakes like that?" His forehead was scrunched, and he looked as if he'd like to wring her neck.

Keep calm. "I didn't want to hit the dog. He ran right out in front of me."

"What dog?" he asked through clenched teeth. "I didn't see any dog." He towered over her.

"It was a big black Lab." Paula refused to back up, even though he looked menacing. She glanced around. "It . . . it's . . . well, it was here a minute ago." Her voice trembled, which made her angry at herself. Why was she nervous? She hadn't done anything wrong, and she had never let any man intimidate her.

7

"Dog or no dog, you should never slam on your brakes like that! Not unless you *want* to get creamed from behind."

"What was I supposed to do? Hit him?" Now Paula was getting angry, too. "It was your fault, anyway. *You* shouldn't have been tailgating."

"Tailgating! I wasn't tailgating."

"You certainly were. I noticed your car two blocks back. It was obvious you were trying to get around me. Why don't you admit it? You were in a hurry and impatient, and you were tailgating! You're just lucky I wasn't seriously hurt!"

His face still looked like thunderclouds, but her statement about not being seriously hurt must have made him think, because he looked at her closely, then said, in a much calmer tone, "Are you *sure* you're all right?"

Paula unclenched her fists and nodded. "Yes. How about you?" Even though his question had been grudging, at least he'd asked, so she felt she could do no less.

"Oh, hell, I'm fine." Disgust tinged his voice. "It's my car that's ruined." He pointed a finger toward the crunched-up spectacle of his formerly shining black BMW, a painful expression on his face.

Paula winced. "I really *am* sorry. Your car definitely got the worst of it." She inclined her head toward the small panel truck she'd been driving. Because it sat higher up off the ground than his car, it had only sustained a broken taillight and dents to the rear door. Although, Paula thought, from the look of the door, she might not be able to open it.

With a loud exhalation of breath, he yanked off his dark, aviator-style sunglasses, and Paula got her first really good look at him.

She sucked in her breath. Movie-star handsome, he had sea-green eyes and silky-looking thick blond hair which complemented his sun-bronzed skin. He reminded her of a sleek, golden jungle cat disguised in gray pinstripes.

Paula suddenly wished she wasn't wearing an ugly blue coverall and dirty sneakers. Automatically her hand reached up to pat her dark, curly hair, and she smiled.

"I just bought that car," he said bitterly.

Paula's smile faded, and she made a sympathetic noise. She supposed if she could afford a BMW, she'd be pretty upset to have it smashed up, too. But she was also pretty sure she wouldn't tailgate while driving it.

He turned to face her once more. His eyes glittered in the sunlight. "I'm glad you weren't hurt, but I hope you learned a lesson from this."

"Me?" Paula squeaked.

"You should never let yourself become distracted from your driving," he continued as if she hadn't spoken.

What was with this guy? Where did he get off lecturing her? *She* hadn't hit *him*. "Well, *you* should learn how to control your vehicle," she retorted. "If you'd been maintaining a safe distance behind me, this never would have happened." Her Italian temper simmered even as she remembered her mother's warning to curb her tongue.

"Men don't like opinionated women," she'd said dozens of times. "They like women who agree with them, who listen to them. And they especially hate women who have to have the last word."

"I really don't care what men think," Paula had answered.

"You'd better start caring," Dot Romano said

darkly. "You're twenty-eight and not getting any younger." Her mother refused to believe that Paula had no interest in marriage, and Paula had given up on trying to convince her.

But her mother's advice faded from Paula's mind as Green-Eyes opened his mouth, then clamped it shut and glared at her.

Paula glared back. She *knew* men didn't like to be told they were wrong, especially when it came to driving. Most of the men Paula knew, including her father, thought only they were capable of operating an automobile the way it was meant to be operated. They always said the words "female driver" as if they were an insult.

Eyes narrowed, her adversary reached into the inside pocket of his dark gray pinstriped suit and whipped out a small, leather-bound notebook and a gold Cross pen. "What's your name?" he asked, the sound as close to a bark as Paula had ever heard.

She fought against the smile trying to emerge. All of a sudden, his fury, the whole situation, struck her as funny. But she knew it would be disastrous to smile. Aside from being told they didn't know how to drive, men hated to be laughed at more than anything. "Paula Romano," she said meekly. "And what's yours?"

From an inner pocket of the notebook he removed a business card, scribbled something on the back, then handed it to her. Their eyes met once more, something flickering in the cool depths of his as they stared at each other.

How could eyes so gorgeous be so cold? she wondered. Didn't Mr. Magnificent ever smile? Didn't he have any sense of humor? She looked down at the card, squinting against the strong sun. CLAYBOURNE, BESKA, SEBASTIAN, AND NORMAN, ATTOR-

NEYS-AT-LAW. Underneath, in smaller letters was neatly printed: Matthew J. Norman, III.

Claybourne, Beska, Sebastian, and Norman! Kim MacAllister, Paula's best friend, worked for this law firm. Paula could hardly wait to get home and call her. Kim would die.

Paula turned the card over. He had written the name of his insurance company and agent on the back.

Matt watched the girl as she read his card, both front and back. He wondered what she was thinking as she looked up again and the full brilliance of her enormous brown eyes settled on his face. He had the uneasy feeling she was secretly amused.

"Here's my insurance card," she said.

Matt accepted the card, his hand brushing against hers in the process. He couldn't help noticing how small and fragile-looking her wrist was. He also took note of the thin gold bangle bracelet, an incongruity with her uniform. Irritated with the direction of his thoughts, he said, "Romano Pool Service? You own a pool-service company?"

"It's my father's company." Her dark eyes continued to watch him, unnerving him with their calm scrutiny. He couldn't picture her working for a pool service. It was an unusual occupation for any woman, but especially one so . . . sexy. The unbidden thought came out of nowhere. What had possessed him to think that? Paula Romano wasn't the type of woman he normally thought of as sexy. He preferred tall, blond, elegant women. Paula Romano was small, dark, and at the opposite end of the spectrum from elegant. Dressed as she was in a blue uniform and running shoes, with clouds of unruly hair flying all over the place in the stiff breeze and a smudge of dirt across her nose, she looked like a refugee from a prison work camp. No.

Definitely not his type. Flustered, he quickly finished copying the information from her insurance card.

Paula continued to study him while he wrote. He certainly was good-looking. Too bad he was so uptight. He looked to be about six feet tall, and his shoulders were broad and his waist narrow. Even the conservative cut of his suit did nothing to disguise the athletic look of his body. He certainly wasn't her idea of what an attorney looked like. Weren't all lawyers stuffy-looking? Didn't they all resemble Woody Allen and wear horn-rimmed glasses and have pale skin from burying themselves in musty law libraries all day long?

"Should we call the police?" she asked helpfully. Maybe if she cooperated instead of arguing with him, he'd loosen up a bit. After all, she could afford to be magnanimous. She knew she was in the right.

"The police no longer come to the scene of traffic accidents." Still no smile.

Was that frown a permanent part of his face? Paula wasn't sure why, but she was beginning to think she'd do anything to see if she could make him smile. In fact, she was beginning to wonder if he *could* smile.

By now they'd attracted a little knot of spectators, and a young boy of about eighteen with spiky red hair and dime-sized freckles said, "That's true, but you don't have to worry. I saw it all. It was definitely his fault." He grinned at Paula, and she grinned back.

Matt saw the exchange of smiles, and for some reason, it only served to irritate him more. He closed his eyes and wondered what he'd done to deserve this aggravation. He wished he were anywhere but here in the middle of one of Houston's busiest streets facing a little know-it-all with dimples and a smart mouth. He sighed. He really wanted to say a few more choice things, not only to her but to the overgrown adolescent drooling all over her, but he pushed the desire away. A wise lawyer knew when to keep quiet, and Matt was a wise lawyer. All he had to do was go back to his car, call a wrecker from his mobile phone, and let his insurance company handle this situation from here on out. In fact, he never had to see this aggravating woman again.

"As soon as I get back to my office, I'll call my insurance company," he said. "They'll be in touch."

"Do you need a ride?" she asked.

"Thank you, but I believe I can manage."

"Are you sure? I'll be glad to take you wherever you want to go."

"I'm perfectly sure."

He turned away, walking toward his car. He still hadn't smiled once.

"I don't think your car is driveable," Paula said as she followed him. Why was he being so stubborn? What did he plan to do—sit there in his car and just hope a wrecker service would magically materialize? Why wouldn't he let her help him?

He stopped abruptly, turning to look at her again. "I know that, Miss Romano. Despite what you may think, I *do* know something about cars and their operation. And I'm perfectly capable of getting myself back to my office. You don't have to wait around."

Paula's jaw hardened. In other words, get lost, Miss Romano. Couldn't he see that she was just trying to be nice? Would it kill him to act like a human being, to smile just one time?

Okay, Old Stone-Face, have it your way, she thought. *Don't be nice. Sit here until hell freezes over. See if I care.*

But she *did* care. It really bothered her that he'd been so unfriendly and so unwilling to bend. And the fact that he wasn't interested enough in her to make any effort to be nice really rankled. Grumbling to herself, she started the truck and drove away from the accident scene. An hour from now he probably would have forgotten her name.

"I wonder just what it would take to get Matthew J. Norman to smile at me?" she said aloud. Then she smiled. That grim face was beginning to feel like a challenge.

And she had never been able to resist a challenge.

Matt Norman threw down the Lambert brief in a spurt of disgust. What was it his mother always said when he felt like this? She'd tell him he took himself far too seriously, that he needed to loosen up and have some fun. Matt rubbed his forehead wearily. Usually, when he was upset, he'd methodically force himself to think about something else. He'd learned long ago how pointless it was to waste his energy on circumstances he couldn't change.

But that irritating girl refused to vanish from his thoughts. Just as he'd almost achieve full concentration on the brief, Bambi Brown Eyes would push her way into his consciousness. She'd thought he was a fool. She'd been laughing at him.

Damn. He *had* been tailgating. He'd been thinking about Lambert Construction Company and whether Michael Lambert was telling him the truth about not having inside information on the new courthouse bids, and he hadn't been paying attention. He'd also been impatient. She was right when she'd said he'd tried to get around her several times before she'd slammed on her brakes. Knowing the Romano girl hadn't caused the accident only irritated him further. Matt wasn't used to being in the wrong, and he didn't like the feeling.

Shake it off, he told himself. *On a scale of one to ten, how important is this accident or the girl? What do you care if some girl you've never seen before and will never see again thinks you're a fool? Let the insurance agent deal with her, and that'll be the end of this episode. Period.* Matt sighed and picked up the Lambert brief, but a small part of his mind refused to relinquish the image of dark, laughing eyes and flashing dimples.

Paula discarded one scenario after another. Some of them were stupid—like showing up on his doorstep wrapped in cellophane with an iced bottle of champagne under her arm. But she couldn't help grinning at the image. His eyes would probably pop just like the champagne cork. But would he smile?

Nothing reasonable came to mind, and all during the rest of the afternoon, as she answered service calls and dodged friendly and not-so-friendly dogs, she thought about how she was going to get Matt Norman's attention. His undivided attention—as well as a smile.

She was still dreaming up nutty schemes at six o'clock that evening when she called Kim.

"You know, Paula. You're crazy," Kim said after Paula gave her a play-by-play description of her encounter with Matt Norman. "Why do you even care what he thinks?"

"I don't, really. It's just that . . . I don't know. I can't explain it."

"You can't explain it because it doesn't make sense. My advice is to forget about him. You wouldn't like him anyway. He's simply not your type. Matt Norman is boring and stuffy and very conservative. The two of you have absolutely nothing in common."

Paula examined her fingernails. "Are you going to help me or not?"

She heard Kim sigh at the other end of the phone. "Do I have a choice?"

"No."

After dire mutterings about friendship and stupidity and fools rushing in, Kim asked, "What do you want to know?"

"All about him. Everything you know."

"I don't know that much. All I am is a paralegal in the domestic division. He's a partner who handles civil cases."

"You must know more than that!"

"He's the grandson of one of the founders of the firm, his father is a senior partner, he's single, and his family is rich, rich, rich. He's not on the same planet as you and me."

"He made that obvious. What about his love life?"

"I don't know anything about his love life."

Paula laughed. "Oh, come on. That law firm of yours is a gossip mill. Everybody knows everything." When Kim stayed silent, Paula prodded. "Does he date anyone at the firm?"

"No. At least not since I've been there. Not that most of the women haven't tried to get him to ask them out—"

"But he never has?"

"Nope. I told you, Paula—he's stuffy. Don't be fooled by his looks. Under that surfer exterior beats the heart of an Establishment snob. He's hell to work for, too; wants everything done just so; a stickler for details; all business; expects you to work all hours."

Paula knew Kim was trying her darndest to dissuade her from pursuing any further involvement with Matt

Norman, but the more Kim talked, the more determined Paula got.

"So," she continued, "you can see what a misdirected waste of effort it would be to try to catch his attention."

"I understand what you're saying, Kim, but it bugs me that he acted the way he did. What would it have cost him to smile? I just want to prove to myself that I can make him notice me. Maybe even get him to ask me for a date."

Kim groaned. "Paula, please forget about him. I have a bad feeling about this. Messing around with the likes of Matt Norman . . . well, it could backfire."

But Paula had never been able to resist a challenge. Absentmindedly, she stroked the thick fur of Miss Milly, her beloved calico cat, whose rumbled purr sounded like a motorboat. "I really don't have a choice," she said softly. "He threw down the gauntlet."

"And you can't resist picking it up," Kim finished.

Miss Milly turned around in circles on the bed, then settled down next to Paula in a contented heap.

"You know me," Paula said.

"Unfortunately, I do. I just wish you'd think about this for a while."

Paula grinned. Kim looked like a *Playboy* centerfold, but her mind worked like an accountant's. She never did anything impulsively. Before she considered dating anyone, she checked him out thoroughly—including his financial status.

"I *am* thinking about it."

"Mark my words, Paula. If you persist in this foolhardy scheme, you're going to get more than you bargained for."

"Thank you. I needed that vote of confidence."

"I give up. Just don't say I didn't warn you. And don't come crying to me when everything goes wrong." Then, as a parting shot, Kim said, "And don't ever let Matt Norman know that you know me. I need my job."

Paula chuckled as they hung up. Then she fed Miss Milly, changed into pink workout clothes, and went to The Waist Basket for the eight o'clock aerobics class. Her mind always worked better when her body was occupied. There was something about sweating that oiled the brain.

Afterward, pleasantly limbered up and feeling virtuous, she went home and tossed an enormous salad with vinegar and oil dressing and kept thinking about The Problem. She still hadn't come up with an idea by bedtime, so she read Sue Grafton's latest novel for a while, then turned out her light and lay in the dark. Miss Milly parked her overweight body next to Paula's hip and settled down for the night.

As Paula lay there, the germ of an idea began, and she toyed with it awhile. Smiling to herself, she rolled over. Miss Milly howled in protest.

"You're a bed hog, you know that?" Paula said soothingly as she rubbed the cat's ears. "I didn't mean to disturb you."

After Paula was once again settled with the cat against her hip, she hugged her pillow in deep contentment and fell asleep.

The next morning she put her plan into action. Picking up the phone, she pressed the numbers to her parents' home. "Hi, Mom," she said when her mother answered. "I thought you'd be gone by now." Her mother worked as a secretary at an elementary school in southwest Houston.

"I was just on my way out when I heard the phone ringing. Something wrong, Paula?"

Paula heard the concern in her mother's voice. A typical Italian mother, Dot Romano worried about her children constantly. And when there wasn't anything real to worry about, she invented things. For the past couple of years, her biggest worry had been finding Paula a suitable husband.

"Nothing's wrong," Paula assured her. "I just wanted to talk to Rocky."

"Rocky's still in bed. He was up half the night studying."

"Well, would you call him? I've got a job for him."

"Oh, good. He needs money."

Paula's nineteen-year-old brother attended the University of Houston and was always looking for ways to earn spending money.

A few minutes later, Rocky's sleep-fogged voice said, "Yeah? What's up, Paul?"

"Want to earn a quick twenty bucks?"

"Sure, long as I don't have to kill anybody."

She ignored his attempt at humor. "Don't worry. I just want you to deliver a letter for me sometime this morning. Can you do that?"

"Where to?"

"Downtown."

"Yeah, sure, I can do it. You gonna bring the letter over here?"

"Yes. I'll drop if off on my way to work. See you in about an hour."

After saying good-bye, Paula sat down at her desk and took out a sheet of her prettiest stationery—pale-blue with a dark-blue scalloped edge—and began writing.

*   *   *

Matt's stomach grumbled and complained. He closed the Millsaps file and stacked it neatly in his "To Be Filed" basket for his secretary, Rachel, to take care of later.

"Ready for lunch?"

Matt looked up as his best friend and co-worker, Rory Sebastian, entered his office. Rory's black eyes gleamed with amusement, and his dark, chiseled face held a smile.

"What're you so happy about?" Matt asked as he stood up.

Rory leaned lazily against the doorframe. "Oh, I was just teasing Rachel."

Matt shook his head. Rory loved women. Old or young, homely or pretty. It made no difference to him. He enjoyed an easy camaraderie with them that Matt envied. They all loved Rory and endured his teasing with smiles and obvious affection.

"I'm starving," Matt said.

"Well, what are we waiting for?" Rory rubbed his flat stomach. "How does red beans and rice sound?"

Matt groaned. The thought of the spicy Cajun dish started his salivary glands working. With a resigned sigh, he said, "I guess that means you want to go to Treebeard's again? So much for a light lunch."

"A growing boy needs more than a salad."

"You quit growing years ago."

"I did?" Rory's dark eyes flashed as they walked through the outer office. Matt's secretary looked up from her computer terminal and grinned as Rory mugged for her.

"We're going to lunch, Rachel. We'll be back about one-thirty," Matt said.

They strolled out the door and down the thickly carpeted hallway toward the reception area. The plush, wine-red carpet; creamy, textured wallpaper; polished walnut desk, and soft leather furniture gracing the reception area never failed to give Matt a surge of pleasure. The room soothed him—its subdued elegance and beauty exactly the right touch for a dignified law firm. A poised, honey-blond beauty sat behind the enormous desk facing the outside doors.

Matt and Rory looked curiously at the dark-haired young man who had pushed open the double glass doors just as they entered the room. Dressed in faded jeans and pullover sweater, his dark, curly hair too long to be fashionable, he carried a skateboard under his left arm.

Rory raised his eyebrows, and Matt shrugged.

"May I help you?" the blonde said to the kid.

He held up a pale-blue envelope. "I have a letter for Mr. Matthew J. Norman the Third."

"Let me see that," Matt said, walking toward him.

The boy hesitated, looking to the receptionist for guidance. "It's marked Personal," he said.

She said, "This is Mr. Norman," and pointed to Matt.

"Oh." The boy handed the envelope to Matt.

Although he never tipped messengers, Matt dug into his pocket and pulled out a couple of dollar bills. "Thanks," he said.

"Thank *you*." Whistling merrily, the boy pushed the doors open and disappeared.

Matt stared at the envelope. There was no return address. His name and the address of the law firm were written in neat, rounded script on the front. In the bottom left-hand corner was printed, URGENT AND PERSONAL.

He frowned. Tearing open the flap, he removed the single sheet of scalloped stationery.

Dear Mr. Norman,

I know you were upset yesterday, and I can't say I blame you. I'm really sorry about your car, and I'd like to make it up to you by taking you to dinner tonight. I'll call you later this afternoon to see what time would be good for you.

Paula Romano

Paula Romano! Make *what* up to him? What the heck was she talking about? The accident had been his fault, and she knew it. In fact, she'd rubbed it in. So what was her game? Matt could feel the other pairs of eyes in the room. He raised his own eyes. Sure enough, both the receptionist and Rory were watching him.

"Bad news?" asked Rory.

"Why do you say that?"

"You have an odd look on your face."

Matt stuffed the offending missive into his jacket pocket and said gruffly, "Come on, let's go eat."

Later, settled in the noisy restaurant with their steaming plates of red beans and rice in front of them, Rory once again raised the subject of the letter. "So . . . are you going to tell me about it or not?" He buttered a piece of the hot, jalapeño cornbread and took a large bite. His eyes held a quizzical gleam.

Matt unhurriedly swallowed and said in an offhand way, "Tell you about what?"

"Don't play possum with me. Remember who you're talkin' to here." Rory pointed to his chest. "This is old Rory. Your buddy. Remember?"

"Oh, all right." Matt reached into his jacket pocket, withdrew the letter, and handed it to Rory. Rory quickly read it, then looked up with a sly grin. "I take it this is the chick who caused you to wreck your car yesterday."

Matt nodded glumly and reached for the hot sauce, sprinkling it liberally over his food. Then he took another fiery bite.

"Well, come on. Tell me about her," Rory coaxed. "It looks like she's interested in you."

"There's nothing to tell. And she's *not* interested in me." She'd laughed at him, but he had no intention of telling Rory that. "And I'm certainly not interested in *her*!"

"I have a feeling you're leaving out something," Rory said. The smile tugging at the corners of his mouth refused to disappear. "Come on, come clean. What's she like? Is she a fox?" He raised his eyebrows and moved his fingers in an imitation of Groucho Marx holding a cigar.

Matt laughed. Rory could always make him laugh. He shrugged. "She's okay. Not my type." He ignored the sudden vision of shapely curves that couldn't be hidden by a baggy coverall; of melting brown eyes and wild, curly brown hair; of deep dimples and an impish smile.

"Just 'okay,' huh? Why do I feel you're not being one hundred percent honest with me, my good man?" Now he used an exaggerated British accent.

Ignoring his friend's theatrics, Matt said, "Why do you say that?" in an innocent voice.

"You had the same odd look on your face just now as you did when you read the letter, that's why." Rory's eyes twinkled.

"You're imagining things."

"I don't think so."

"Damn you, Rory. Wipe that smile off your face."

The smile became bigger, and Rory leaned back in his chair. He didn't say anything.

Matt threw his napkin down. "All right. Maybe I

wasn't entirely honest with you. She's . . . fairly attractive in a small, dark, intense kind of way. But she's not my type. And I don't trust that note. She has some ulterior motive in inviting me out to dinner, but I'm not sure what it is."

"Maybe the note is just what it appears to be. Maybe she's just trying to be nice . . . make it up to you because of your car."

"Maybe." Matt took a large swallow of his iced tea.

"So you're refusing the dinner invitation, right?"

"Right." When Rory didn't respond, Matt shifted in his chair. "I don't trust her, and I'm not interested in her, so there's no reason to see her again. Why invite trouble?"

"Hey," Rory said, raising his hands in mock surrender. "Did I say anything?" Then, under his breath, he muttered, "Methinks he doth protest too much."

"I heard that," Matt said. "And I know exactly what you're thinking, but you're wrong."

"Okay. You've convinced me."

"Then why do you still have that stupid grin on your face?"

TWO

Promptly at four o'clock Paula found a pay phone and called Matt's office.

"Claybourne, Beska, Sebastian, and Norman," purred a silken voice.

Paula pictured the girl belonging to the voice. Tall. Slinky. Sultry. Long, long, legs and designer hair. She definitely wouldn't be wearing sneakers to work.

"Matthew J. Norman the Third, please," Paula said in her best ex-schoolteacher voice.

"Who's calling, please?"

"Paula Romano."

"One moment, please."

The soothing sounds of easy-listening music floated through the receiver as Paula waited for him to come on the line.

"Matt Norman."

Paula smiled. "Hello, Mr. Norman. Did you get my letter?"

"Oh." A pause. "Miss Romano. Yes, I received your letter. But I'm afraid I can't take you up on your invitation."

Cool. Remote. Her smile broadened. He really thought he could just brush her off. *Think again, Mr. Norman.* "I'm terribly disappointed," she said softly. "I'd like us to be friends."

"That's very kind of you, Miss Romano—"

"Oh, please call me Paula."

"—Paula." He sounded reluctant to say the word.

"And are you called Matthew or Matt?"

"Uh . . . Matt."

"I thought so. Matt suits you." She waited a heartbeat. "Are you positive you can't make it tonight?"

"I wish I could, but I have a lot of work to take home."

"But you still have to eat." It was hot inside the phone booth. With the toe of her sneaker, she nudged the phone booth door open to let some air in.

"Look, Miss Romano, I appreciate your concern, but you have no reason to feel as if you have to make something up to me. We both know the accident was my fault. Now, if you don't mind, I'm terribly busy—"

"Paula."

"What?"

"Paula. Call me Paula. Not Miss Romano."

There was a long silence. "Paula." For a brief moment, she thought she'd won, that he was going to have a change of heart, but instead he said, "Well . . . Paula . . . thanks again . . . and good-bye."

The click told her he'd broken the connection.

Paula listened to the sound of the open telephone line buzzing in her ear. She chuckled in remembrance of his obvious discomfort. "Matthew J. Norman," she said aloud as she walked to her truck parked nearby. "Don't think you've seen the last of me. This is just the end of Round One. Round Two is coming up."

All the way back to the pool repair company's head-quarters, she plotted. Bypassing the company's reception area, she entered through the warehouse and waved hello to the other two servicemen, Brian and Eddie.

"Hey, how's it goin' today, Paula?" called Eddie.

"Great," she said, and pushed open the door leading to her father's small, cluttered office. Frank Romano, a short, dark man with salt-and-pepper hair and eyes the exact color of Paula's, looked up.

"Hi, honey." His weathered face creased into a broad smile.

Paula bent down to drop a kiss on his forehead. "Hi, Dad."

"Have a good day?" He reached into his shirt pocket and extracted a crumpled pack of Marlboro Lights.

She dropped into the beat-up leather chair in front of his desk. "It wasn't bad . . . I didn't have any problems." Matt Norman's male-model face drifted through her mind.

Her father took a deep drag on his cigarette and blew the smoke out in perfect rings. "Something's bothering you, though," he said thoughtfully.

Paula knew she wore her emotions on her face most of the time, but she and her father had always had that special closeness that couldn't be rationally explained. "I wish you'd quit smoking," she said.

He grinned. "Is that a non sequitur, or is that what's bothering you?"

Paula picked up a paper clip from the edge of his desk and threw it at him. They both laughed. She loved her sharply intelligent, understanding father. How many other fathers would be so sympathetic . . . so nonjudgmental if their only daughter, after completing five years of college and earning a master's degree in music, decided after only two years of teaching music that she couldn't stand what she was doing? Paula would never forget the day she'd told him. She had agonized over her decision for weeks and finally just blurted it out.

"So you hate being cooped up all day, and you really want a career as a performer."

"Yes," she said, heart jumping madly. She hated disappointing him.

"Well, I'm not surprised," he said with a smile.

A great surge of relief flowed through Paula. She should have known he'd understand. She returned his smile weakly.

"Why don't you just keep on working for me?" he suggested. "That way you can take time off anytime you have a part."

"Really? You mean it?" Joy shot through her in heady spurts. She'd worked summers in his pool business since she was a junior in high school.

"We can work your schedule around rehearsals and performances."

"Oh, Dad! I love you!" Paula threw her arms around him.

"Now, let's not get emotional," he said gruffly. "I've got an ulterior motive anyway, you know." He disengaged her arms and held her at arm's length, his eyes full of love. "I'm counting on you to become rich and famous and support me in my old age."

"You'll never be sorry," she promised, eyes misty.

And ever since that day three years ago, he'd never indicated by so much as a look that he was sorry. One of these days, she thought, his confidence in her would pay off, even though she had decided about a year ago that the performing end of the music business probably wasn't her strong point. For the past year her efforts had been concentrated on composing, and she finally felt as if this was what she was meant to do. She knew she'd picked a hard profession to break into, but—she grinned to herself—when had she ever let a little challenge stop her?

The telephone on her father's desk buzzed, startling Paula out of her reverie.

"Yeah," he said into the receiver. "Hi, hon." *It's your mother*, he mouthed.

Paula nodded. She absently picked up a brochure about pool chemicals and leafed through it, idly wondering if Matt Norman had a pool. She had a sudden, clear vision of what he'd look like in snug bathing trunks. *Oh, Paula, you've been without a boyfriend too long.*

"Okay, okay," her father said.

Paula looked up. He grinned and wrinkled his nose at something her mother was saying. "'Sure. She's right here. I will. Okay. See you later." He replaced the receiver. "Your mother said to invite you for dinner. Tony and Susan are coming, and they're bringing take-out Chinese." Tony was one of Paula's four brothers, and Susan was his wife.

Paula loved Chinese food. She also loved Susan. Tony she wasn't sure about. Like her mother and the rest of her family, he was always telling her what to do. None of them understood her. Her father was the only member of her family who allowed her to be herself. That was probably why she was so stubborn.

She opened her mouth to say "yes" when suddenly she knew what she would do for Round Two. "Sounds tempting, Dad, but I can't. I've got a date."

She hurried home, showered and washed her hair, and while it was drying naturally, she pulled out the telephone directory. She ran her finger down the "N's." Good heavens. There were over a hundred Normans listed. But there he was, right after Norman,

Mary. Norman, Matthew J., III, 5434 Bayou Trail. She pulled out her key map. Bayou Trail wasn't all that far from her town house. Maybe a fifteen-minute drive.

Paula looked at the clock. It was already six-thirty. She'd have to get a move on. She plugged in her curling iron, and while it was heating, she carefully made up her face and studied herself in the bathroom mirror.

Although her face was a well-shaped oval, and she had a nice, straight nose and good skin, Paula thought her face was boring. If only she looked like Kim with her auburn hair that she wore short and sleek, and her royal-blue eyes. Paula also hated her dimples, and her hair drove her crazy. She sighed. She couldn't change the way she looked; she'd just have to make the best of what she had.

Using the curling iron to force her hair to go the direction she wanted it to go, she sprayed it, then rooted through her closet, discarding one outfit after another until she came to her white gabardine jump suit. Perfect. After adding a narrow brown alligator belt and matching high-heeled shoes, she was satisfied. Smiling at her image, she added her gold bangle bracelet and big gold hooped earrings, spritzed herself with Shalimar, and said aloud, "Get out your gloves, Matt Norman, 'cause I'm on my way."

After his conversation with Paula, Matt thought of six dozen other things he could have said and didn't. Well, at least he hadn't lied to her. He *did* have a tremendous amount of work to do, and he *was* planning to take it all home with him. And after the enormous lunch he'd had today, the last thing he needed was a heavy dinner.

He switched on his dictating equipment. He might as

well get as much done here at the office as he could. He picked up the Millsaps file and began dictating.

At five o'clock there was a soft tap on his door.

"Yes?"

The door opened. A svelte blonde with a mocking smile strolled in. "Hi, Matt," she drawled. "Still at it, I see."

He groaned inwardly. Jill Carmichael was one of the newest lawyers to be hired by the firm, and he'd made a big mistake by asking her out a few weeks before. He'd made it a policy never to date anyone who worked for the firm, and he'd stuck to it—until Jill. But he'd been at a low point, and she was just the type of woman who had always attracted him, so he'd given in to the temptation to take her out.

Matt had always planned to marry when he was about thirty-five or thirty-six, and he knew it was time to begin seriously looking for the right candidate. Jill Carmichael had looked promising. She was poised. Beautiful. Intelligent. Someone he'd be proud to be seen with. She would know what fork to use and how to talk to his colleagues and friends. The fact that she was a lawyer was a drawback, but not a serious one. Actually, once he thought about it, he realized that although he would never want a wife who practiced law, it might be nice to have one who understood what he was talking about.

But he'd known after one date it was a go-nowhere relationship. Jill was ambitious and smart; she'd worked like a demon to put herself through law school, and she had plans for herself. She'd made that abundantly clear—in fact, sometimes Matt wondered if she was really interested in him, the person, or in Matthew J. Norman, the associate who was probably next in line for a senior partnership—a man who could save her years of hard work in her climb up the ladder.

Matt had no interest in a career woman like Jill. Ever since he'd been old enough to think about it, he'd known he wanted a traditional, stay-at-home wife, one who would put him and his needs first. But for some reason—probably inertia, he thought ruefully, or maybe just plain hormones—he'd continued to date Jill, even as he'd berated himself for giving in to this weakness.

He'd been lucky. So far, he didn't think anyone at the office, except Rory, knew they were dating, but sooner or later they'd get wind of it, and that would be a disaster. Especially since he knew he wasn't seriously interested in her. The last thing he wanted to do was hurt Jill in any way. She was really very nice, but not for him.

"Hello, Jill," he said, enjoying the perfection of her beauty even as he told himself he had to quit seeing her.

Gliding to his desk, she leaned over it to give him a warm, lingering kiss. Her musky perfume enveloped him as she perched on a corner of his desk, pushing his calendar and pen holder out of the way. She cocked her head and studied him, a small smile lifting the corners of her mouth. "I came to rescue you from yourself. You've worked late every night for the past week. It's time to relax a little."

Matt stifled the small surge of irritation at her proprietary action. He pointedly straightened both the calendar and the pen holder as he said, "I'm swamped, Jill. I'll probably be working all night to catch up."

She ran her hand slowly down his cheek. "Can't I persuade you to forget work for tonight? I had an idea we could pick up some nice thick juicy steaks and go to

your house and fix dinner and . . ." Her voice lowered
seductively.

He started to refuse. He hated any disruption of his
planned agenda. He also hated women who tried to
manipulate him. But this evening *would* give them an
opportunity to talk, and he could make it clear to Jill
that although he liked her immensely, he thought it best
that they sever their relationship. He would say it in
the nicest way, of course. He would present his case
reasonably and quietly. Jill, being sensible and intelligent, would agree, and they would part friends. There
would be no messy scene, another thing Matt despised.
Satisfied with his decision, he smiled and said,
"You've talked me into it. I've been wanting to talk
to you anyway."

It was exactly seven-thirty when Paula pulled up in
front of 5434 Bayou Trail. The sun had gone down,
and a hazy purple light still lingered over the warm
Houston night. The air was filled with muted sounds:
children playing, dogs barking, mothers calling out,
birds fluttering through the trees, a car engine, and
somewhere farther along the wooded, winding street,
the hollow smack of tennis balls. Paula took a deep
breath. She could smell the woodsy aroma of barbecue
and the heady perfume of autumn roses and pine
needles.

The house was just the kind of place she would have
expected Matt Norman to live in. A low California-
style contemporary—all natural wood and stone and
glass—tucked into the sheltering pines and tall oaks.
Paula knew Buffalo Bayou meandered behind the
house, and she could imagine the spectacular view Matt
would have.

As she walked up the cobbled sidewalk, she struggled to hold on to the moo shu pork, lemon chicken, hot and sour soup, spring rolls, and plum wine.

Paula pressed the doorbell and waited, admiring the azalea bushes flanking his front door. She pressed the doorbell again. She could hear the faint chimes inside. Still no answer. She nibbled on her bottom lip. Maybe he hadn't come home yet.

Just as she was ready to leave in temporary defeat, the door opened, and Matt Norman stood there. His eyes widened.

"Hello, Matt," she said softly.

His mouth dropped open in total disbelief.

"I felt sorry for you with all that work to do, so I thought I'd surprise you and bring dinner here." Paula gave him what she hoped was her sexiest, most appealing smile.

"I don't believe this." He looked around helplessly.

"Aren't you going to invite me in?" Paula asked innocently. Look at him squirm.

"Miss Romano—"

"Who is it, Matt?" someone called from inside.

As he turned around, a tall blonde with dark-blue eyes sidled in beside him in the doorway. She wore a plain white silk blouse and a slim navy skirt that ended about two inches above her knees, showing an expanse of long legs that Paula would have killed to own. She stared at Paula. "What's going on?"

Paula stared back, momentarily at a loss when confronted with this unexpected development. What should she do? She could turn tail and run, but why should she? He was the one who had lied about having to work tonight. She kept her voice silky and innocent-sounding. "Hello, there. I'm Paula Romano, a new friend of Matt's." She gave Matt a coy look. "You haven't told her about me?"

The blonde's eyes widened. Paula stood tall. Well, as tall as she could stand, considering she measured exactly five feet two inches.

"What are you doing here?" Matt said. Then he turned to the girl. "I don't have any idea what's going on or what she's talking about."

Paula almost said, "It's all a mistake. Forget it." But she realized she'd come too far to retreat. The damage had already been done. She might as well brazen this out. Furthermore, he *had* lied. He'd said he had too much work to go out to dinner. Why hadn't he had the guts to say straight out that he had a date? He deserved everything he was going to get. From her, *and* from his blond girlfriend.

She raised her chin, smiled sweetly, and said, "When we talked on the phone this afternoon, I understood you to say . . ." She purposely let her voice trail off and backed up a step. "But don't let me spoil your evening. I'll leave." The tantalizing smell of Chinese food drifted between them.

"Now just a minute—" His eyes hardened into glittering emeralds in the dusky light.

Paula backed up another step. "No. It's all right. I understand." She smiled to show him she forgave him. "We'll just do it another time."

"Another time!" he exclaimed.

"Another time!" the blonde said.

Turning, Paula unhurriedly walked down the sidewalk to her car. She really wanted to run. Maybe she'd gone too far. That glint in his eyes had frightened her a bit. After all, what did she really know about Matt Norman? He could have murderous tendencies. But damn him, he deserved it. If he hadn't been such a coward on the phone earlier, if he'd told her the truth, acted like a human being instead of a cold robot, she never would have shown up to interrupt his little love nest. So let him stew and figure out what he was going to tell Goldilocks.

As if on cue, the girl said, "Matt, what the hell is going on here?"

"Later," he said. "I'll explain later. Go inside, Jill. I'll be back in a minute."

"But—"

"No buts. Just go inside," he ordered in an uncompromising voice.

Oh, oh. Paula opened the door of her red Toyota, hoping to escape before he reached her, but just as she turned to get in, a hard hand clamped down on her forearm.

"Oh, no you don't. You're not getting off that easily. Just what's your game?"

Paula winced. Her heart pounded, and she swallowed slowly as she looked up into his eyes. The two of them were standing directly under a streetlamp. They stared at each other for long moments. His eyes were hard and bright and angry. Then his gaze dropped to Paula's mouth, which she was sure was hanging open. For once, she was speechless.

"Cat got your tongue?" he said.

"I . . . I . . ." For the life of her, she couldn't think of a thing to say.

"I think you owe me an explanation. And you're not leaving until I get it."

His dictatorial tone stiffened her spine. "I don't have to explain one single thing to you," she said defiantly.

"Look, *Miss Romano*, this little stunt you pulled tonight was not only embarrassing, it was loony tunes. What the hell did you think you were doing?"

They stood only inches apart. Both his hands held her upper arms, and she could feel the warmth emanating from his body and smell the woodsy cologne he wore. Heart still pounding like a tom-tom, she wet her lips.

His eyes followed her tongue, and she could feel her face grow hot.

"I was trying to get you to smile," she said.

He dropped his hands as if she'd burned him. "What?"

"Do you know how to smile?" she said.

"Are you crazy?" he countered.

"I don't think so." But she had to admit, if only to herself, that tonight's episode was just about the craziest she'd ever been involved in.

He ran his hands through his hair, mussing the perfect styling. "What is it about you, Paula Romano? Do you invite disaster to follow you around?"

Oh, he was impossible. Paula felt like stamping her foot, but she knew that would be a very childish thing to do, so instead she took a deep breath and said, "I was just trying to be nice. I went to a lot of trouble, not to mention expense, to buy a nice dinner and bring it over here because I believed you when you said you had so much work to do. And what happens? I find out you're not only stuffy and stodgy and uptight and cold, a sourpuss who can't or won't smile, but you're also a coward and a liar!"

He raised his eyebrows. "Is that so?" he said. "Well, for your information, Miss Romano, in my experience, a gentleman tries to spare a lady's feelings. I don't call that lying."

Paula's face burned, and she was glad there wasn't enough light for him to see her discomfiture.

"You *are* a lady, aren't you?" he taunted.

With a wordless sputter of fury, she kicked him. Then she wished the earth would open up and swallow her. He was the one who was supposed to lose his cool. Not her.

He didn't even flinch. "Well, I guess we've settled that question."

"Of course you'd try to make this look like my fault. Why couldn't you just tell me you had a date?" Tired of holding the bags of food, Paula dumped them on top of the car. Then she put her hands on her hips and glared at him.

"Are you sure you want me to answer that question?" he asked quietly.

His composure made her even more furious. "You can't answer it. There *is* no answer that won't make you look like a jerk!"

"All right," he said. "If you insist. The reason I didn't tell you I had a date when you called is that when you called, I didn't *have* a date. It was only after I talked to you that Jill and I decided to spend the evening together."

She almost slapped him. "You *are* a jerk," she said contemptuously. "I don't know why I ever thought it was worth wasting time on you." Tears welled in her eyes, but she blinked them back angrily. Dot Romano always said men hated tears, and even though Paula never paid any attention to her mother's outdated ideas, she wouldn't give Matt Norman the satisfaction of knowing he'd made her cry. She'd die first. She yanked open the car door, grabbed the bags of food and plopped them on the passenger seat, then scrambled into the car.

"Paula—"

"Good night, Mr. Norman." She slammed the door shut, started the car, and sped away. But she couldn't resist a peek into the rearview mirror, and she could see him standing there, under the streetlight, watching her until she turned the corner.

Later that evening as she lay in bed stuffed with Chinese food and plum wine, she felt much better. Dot Romano always said a good meal would banish the blues, and Paula had been in a blue funk for hours. But she hated to admit her mother was right.

The thing was, she was beginning to think she'd made an ass of herself. Why had she gone over there? What had seemed like a good idea had backfired—totally. Instead of embarrassing him, instead of softening him up for the kill, she'd managed to come off looking juvenile and pushy. And in front of that blonde, too. And how could an obviously successful, halfway intelligent man—and he had to be intelligent to get through law school, didn't he?—like Matt Norman prefer an obvious airhead centerfold like Jill to a mature, capable, intelligent woman like Paula?

Oh, forget all about him, she told herself as Miss Milly rubbed up against her. *Forget your goofy scheme to get his attention. Forget that he made you look like an immature fool. Forget that he insinuated that you aren't a lady.*

Soon she was once more seething, and it was a long time before she could fall asleep. Once she finally did, she dreamed she was on a tropical island, lying on hot white sand and listening to the rhythm of the waves breaking on the shore a few feet away. Palm trees swayed overhead, and lush, colorful flowers bloomed in riotous profusion all around her. She could smell the sweet, oily odor of suntan lotion and hear the squawk of sea gulls. Someone began to spread hot lotion over her back with slow, lazy strokes. Her limbs grew heavier, her breathing more shallow. When she turned to see whose hands were working such magic, she wasn't the least surprised to see Matt Norman's glittering green eyes smiling down at her. And when his hot mouth claimed hers, she embraced the dream, and her subconscious self didn't ever want to wake up.

Nothing had gone right since he'd met that damned girl. First he'd overslept. He never overslept! Then it had started to rain. He hated rain. Then his stupid Fiat wouldn't start—the car he was forced to drive because his BMW was in the shop—and he'd had to call his mechanic, then wait for him to come out to the house.

And if all that weren't bad enough, on the way to work he'd gotten a speeding ticket. He hadn't had a speeding ticket since he was nineteen years old. It was all her fault.

But even as he told himself this, he felt like a heel. And why he should feel guilty because some nutty girl had taken it into her head to buy him dinner and bring it over to his house last night, he didn't know. But he did. He couldn't wipe away the picture of the wounded look in her dark eyes when he'd taunted her and told her he hadn't had a date when he'd turned down her dinner invitation.

Damn it. She'd deserved what had happened last night. There was no reason for him to feel sorry for her. She was a big girl; she could take care of herself.

Was he really stodgy and stuffy?

She'd accused him of not knowing how to smile. She'd inferred that he was stiff and dull. She'd called him a coward. A liar. On top of all that, because she'd come to the house, she'd caused all sorts of problems for him with Jill. His carefully thought-out plan of what he would say to Jill was blown to smithereens by Paula's appearance. After Paula left, Jill refused to believe Paula had nothing to do with his desire to terminate their relationship. What should have been a quiet, dignified ending between friends had turned into a stormy argument—one that left Matt wishing he'd never set eyes on either woman.

Blast Paula! Why couldn't she have just left him alone? Then this fiasco wouldn't have happened. Now, without any of this being his fault, he'd hurt the feelings of two women and he felt lower than a snake.

What should he do? Apologize to both of them? What good would that do? He knew if he tried to apologize to Paula, if he did one thing to make it up to her for last night, she'd just take it as a sign that he was interested in her. Then he'd never be rid of her. That he didn't need.

But by three o'clock that afternoon, he knew he wasn't going to be able to forget last night's episode. Paula's jeering voice, the words she'd used to describe him, the glint of angry tears in her eyes—all combined to rob him of his peace of mind and his concentration. Added to that was the knowledge that Jill was probably sitting in her office seething. And he'd have to see her every day.

Sighing heavily, he tapped his pen against the polished surface of his mahogany desk and considered his options. Finally he pressed his intercom.

"Rachel?"

"Yes, Mr. Norman?"

"Rachel, would you call Country Village Florists for me?"

"Certainly, Mr. Norman."

"And buzz me when you've got them on the line."

"Yes, sir."

Twenty minutes later he threw the Brownlee file down in exasperation. He'd read the same paragraph four times and still didn't know what it said. He heartily wished he'd never set eyes on Paula Romano. He knew he was going to regret sending her flowers. He had a strong feeling he'd just invited trouble back into his life.

Trouble with a capital "P" and big brown eyes.

THREE

Paula's head throbbed in time to the windshield wipers. It had been raining steadily all day. Normally, on rainy days, she stayed inside and got caught up on the company's paperwork. But today she'd been forced to go out on two emergency calls, which meant she'd had to grub around in the wet, miserable weather, a fact that hadn't improved her cross temper. She was tired, dirty, had wet feet, and felt like screaming.

To really top off her day, she was now caught in a snarl of traffic on the Katy Freeway. Two of the three out-bound lanes were shut down for repairs, and the always-heavy traffic on this major west side artery came to a virtual standstill while the cars funneled into the one remaining lane.

To keep from going crazy, Paula turned on her tape recorder and worked on lyrics for a new song. When she'd first decided to forget about performing, she had thought she'd miss it, but she didn't. She still performed occasionally—singing at weddings and parties—and last year she'd been invited to sing the national anthem at an Oilers game. Even though her

43

mother wished Paula had never given up teaching, she *did* like to brag about that.

When Paula first started writing songs, she'd concentrated on pop music, but lately she'd been trying her hand at writing country-music ballads, and found she loved it. The song she was working on now was about men who lied, saying one thing when they meant another. In Paula's experience, that probably covered most men. Why was it, she wondered, that women were so open and honest in their relationships, and men were so downright sneaky?

Finally the traffic began moving again. But even after she got back to the office and settled into the paperwork, her day didn't improve. She discovered her father had forgotten to mail the last quarterly tax payment. It was now over three weeks late. She sighed in exasperation. He'd always said keeping books wasn't his strong point.

As she dredged her way through the remaining stack of papers, she listlessly wondered what she'd do that night. The best thing would be to take some aspirin, make herself some hot tea, and spend her evening curled up with her new Mary Higgins Clark novel.

Then she grinned. Maybe she'd pamper herself even more—throw her scruples out the window and order a huge double-cheese, double-mushroom pizza and wash it down with a bottle of Asti Spumante. But then she thought about her self-indulgence of the night before—all that Chinese food and plum wine—and decided her waistline wouldn't forgive her for two such nights in a row. Better eat a container of yogurt and forget the pizza.

When Paula arrived home she sorted through the day's mail and scratched Miss Milly's ears. She'd already kicked off her sneakers and was halfway to her bedroom to change clothes when her doorbell pealed.

"Damn," she muttered. Hurriedly rebuttoning her uniform, she turned and strode to the front door. Peering out the peephole, she saw a young boy with a large basket of flowers in his hands.

"Delivery for Miss Paula Romano," he said when she opened the door.

Curious, Paula accepted the basket. The fragrant scent of carnations and roses filled her nostrils. "Thank you," she said. Setting the basket on the coffee table, she found her wallet and tipped the boy two dollars, then pushed the door shut and slowly walked over to the flowers. The basket held dozens of pink and white carnations, velvety, raspberry-colored roses, and clouds of tiny baby's breath. Glossy leaves and airy fern completed the illusion of springtime.

Frowning, Paula opened the envelope that had been tucked into the arrangement and removed the tiny card. She stared at the message. *I'm sorry about last night. If the invitation's still open, maybe we could go to dinner tonight. Matt Norman.*

Paula bit her lip. *Well, I'll be damned.* She wasn't sure how she felt about the note or Matt Norman. She wondered what she should do. Was he expecting her to call him? It would serve him right if she tossed the flowers in the trash and simply ignored him. Her whole scheme had been stupid anyway. Plus, her life was too busy to fool around playing games with someone as stuffy as he was. As she stood there thinking, the telephone buzzed.

"Paula?" he said when she answered.

Play it very cool. "Yes?" Good. She sounded remote and sophisticated.

"This is Matt Norman."

"Yes, I know."

"Uh . . . did you get the flowers?"

"Yes, I did." She waited, counted to ten, then said in the same remote voice, "They're lovely. Thank you."

"Good. Well, how do you feel about dinner tonight?"

"Why?"

"Why?"

She refused to take pity on him. Men like Matt Norman always had things go their way. It would be good for him to squirm a bit. "That's what I said, Matt. Why? Have you decided you want to be friends? Or are you simply trying to assuage your conscience? Because if it's the latter, I'm not interested."

He was silent for a long time. Finally he said, "I'm really not sure why, Paula. In fact, it's probably a bad idea. Let's just forget it."

She made up her mind quickly. "Dinner sounds very nice," she said sweetly. "What time will you pick me up?"

Matt wondered why he'd invited her to dinner. Had he lost his mind? Why hadn't he just sent her the damned flowers with an apology and closed the door on anything else? What was wrong with him? He knew good and well she wasn't his type.

He'd never been interested in dark, fiery women— the kind who got all passionate about causes and did all sorts of noisy, impetuous things. And now that he was thirty-three years old with an agenda that called for marriage and a family, why waste his time on someone like Paula Romano? The kind of woman he wanted to marry would be cool, elegant, and working in a suitable career that she'd be willing to give up when

she became pregnant. Also—and this was a big also—
after observing how his mother manipulated his father,
Matt had decided that when he married he wanted a
wife who would let him be the boss.

Paula Romano was the bossy kind.

So since she wasn't the kind of woman he wanted
to get involved with on any sort of permanent basis, he
should have just let things alone.

He groaned. Why had he asked her out? He drummed
his fingers on his desk, then swiveled around in his
chair and stared out the window at Houston's imposing
skyline. The rain had finally stopped. A hesitant sun
peeked around the remaining clouds.

An inner voice said, "You know why you invited
her to dinner. You just don't want to admit it. You're
attracted to her."

She *was* a little spitfire, he had to admit that. A sexy
spitfire. He grinned, remembering how she'd looked
when she'd kicked him. At the time he'd wanted to
throttle her, but now, thinking about it, he chuckled
out loud.

Amused with himself, he made a few revisions to
the letters Rachel had typed earlier, then gathered up
his things. He glanced at his watch. Six o'clock. He
had just enough time to dash home and take a quick
shower before their dinner date.

He grabbed his raincoat and walked out the door.
Striding rapidly down the hall, he rounded a corner and
almost knocked his father down.

"Matt!" exclaimed the senior Mr. Norman. "What
fire are you racing off to?"

"Sorry, Dad. I've got a date, and I'm in a hurry."

Matthew J. Norman, II, raised his eyebrows. His
green eyes, so like Matt's own, held a hopeful glimmer.
"Anyone important?"

Matt sighed. "No, Dad. Don't get your hopes up."

"When are you going to settle down, Matt? Aren't you tired of dating? I'd like to have grandchildren someday," he grumbled.

"I'm not your only child," Matt retorted. "Talk to Elizabeth, why don't you?"

"Your sister is worse than you are," the elder Norman complained "Off God-knows-where in some god-forsaken African village. I don't think she'll ever get married."

"I thought you were proud of Elizabeth for working in that jungle hospital."

"I am. I am. But still . . . enough is enough."

Matt smiled. He and Elizabeth weren't carrying out their obligation as proper Normans—their obligation to be fruitful and multiply. He looked at his father. There were dark circles under his eyes, and his normally placid face seemed older and more lined than it had even a couple of weeks ago. A big man with thick, graying hair, his father had put on weight lately, Matt thought. He's sixty-three, and he looks tired. The knowledge saddened Matt. Guilt mixed with love softened his voice. "I want to get married, Dad. I just haven't met the right girl yet."

"What about Sarah?"

Matt heard the hopeful note. Sarah Whittaker was the daughter of old family friends. "Dad, Sarah's like a sister."

"You could do a lot worse."

"Look, I really am running late. Can we have this discussion tomorrow?" He knew without turning around that his father was still standing there watching him as he hurried out the door.

At seven-thirty he was ringing Paula's doorbell. She lived in a quiet area right off the Katy Freeway not too far from his house, and her townhouse complex was neatly tended and shaded by older trees. There were a couple of kids playing soccer in the middle of the cul-de-sac at the end of the block, and their noisy laughter made Matt smile.

The door opened.

Paula stood in the doorway, eyes bright, a smile tugging at the corners of her mouth, giving just a hint of her enchanting dimples.

Matt took a deep breath, then let it out slowly. "Hello, Paula," he said softly.

"Hi, Matt. You're right on time." Then she really did smile.

Matt couldn't help it. He smiled back. She looked sensational. She was wearing a red dress in some kind of silky, flowing material that clung when she turned to get her purse. The full skirt swirled around her legs as she stepped out onto the stoop and locked the door. Then she turned toward him again, and he got a good look at the low V neck and the creamy-looking skin that was exposed. Her small, full breasts were clearly outlined and a single strand of pearls lay just above their swell.

She walked slightly ahead of him to the Fiat parked at the curb, and Matt admired the view of her slender neck and graceful figure. She'd put her thick hair up, twisted it into a topknot, but curly strands escaped all around. She looked like someone's modern-day version of the Gibson Girl—sexy and demure at the same time.

As Matt helped her into the passenger seat, he got a whiff of her perfume and the scent of clean, healthy girl. Something knotted inside him as she swung her slim legs into the car. She was wearing black suede shoes that were all straps and skinny high heels—the kind that made a woman's legs look good enough to take a bite out of.

As he eased away from the curb, he said, "I've made reservations at Brennan's for eight o'clock."

She smiled again, and Matt found himself smiling back. Maybe tonight would turn out to be okay after all.

Paula wasn't sure what she'd expected, but it certainly wasn't this polite, attentive man sitting opposite her. From the moment she'd opened her door and seen him standing on her front stoop dressed in a dark-blue suit, smelling spicy and clean and smiling at her—actually smiling at her—with a heart-stopping, knock-your-socks-off-smile, the evening hadn't been anything like she'd thought it would be.

When they arrived at the restaurant they were whisked to a window table overlooking the enclosed courtyard. Soft lamps cast an intimate glow over the faces of the diners, and Paula sank into her chair with a contented sigh. The waiter hovered nearby as Matt studied the wine list.

The cool, crisp wine, the hushed voices around them, the quiet elegance of the restaurant, the succulent turtle soup, the rich blend of shrimp and scallops, the sinfully delicious Bananas Foster—a specialty of the restaurant—all combined to lull Paula into imagining she was in the middle of a dream. Then her face felt hot, because she remembered her real dream, the one where she and Matt were on that island and he'd made hot, passionate love to her.

To distract herself, she said, "This was a wonderful dinner, Matt. I enjoyed it."

He smiled. The smile really did change his face, she thought. He looked so much more relaxed, so much more like a real person instead of a model for suntan lotion. And this was about the tenth time he'd smiled tonight. Paula could hardly believe it. The other times she'd been in his company, he hadn't smiled once. Now here he was, smiling and acting human and . . . nice.

Paula had planned to pay the bill. But now she wasn't sure if she should. If Matt had acted arrogant or nasty, she would have grabbed the bill and kept total control of the situation, but he'd been so . . . sweet. He acted as if he liked her, as if this were a real date between two people who wanted to be together. How could she embarrass him when he was trying so hard?

As she sat there stewing, the waiter approached and discreetly laid the leather folder next to Matt.

Paula made up her mind. Tonight she was calling a truce. Depending on the way he acted for the rest of the evening, she might even call an end to her scheme. Maybe she'd been unfair to him from the very beginning.

"Ready?" he said, smiling again.

Good grief, if he kept smiling at her like that, she might even *like* him. And wouldn't Kim laugh about that?

They walked through the back dining room and out toward the front of the restaurant. Matt tried to ignore Paula's seductive little bottom as she gracefully walked ahead of him. Just as they were passing the large dining room facing the street, someone called, "Matt!"

Paula stopped. Matt's head swiveled around, and his eyes settled on the surprised faces of his father and mother. Matt's heart sank. He wanted to turn around and pretend he hadn't seen them, but he knew that was impossible. He took Paula's arm and led her forward, into the dining room.

"Hello, Mom, Dad."

His father stood up. Matt glanced down at their table. They'd just been served dessert and coffee.

"Join us," his mother invited, her eyes bright and interested, slyly looking Paula over.

Matt shook his head. "No, no. We're finished. We were just leaving," he added unnecessarily.

His mother laughed, the sound tinkling and merry. "I can *see* that, but I never get to see you anymore, darling. You're always too busy. Come on. Sit down and introduce me to this young lady."

Matt groaned inwardly, but what choice did he have? He drew Paula forward. His father signaled their waiter.

"We need two more chairs," his father said. The waiter responded immediately, and before Matt realized how it had all happened, he and Paula were seated at the table.

His mother extended her hand to Paula. "I'm Betty Norman, Matt's mother." Her gray eyes sparked with interest as she studied Paula. As usual, his mother looked lovely—her slim body elegant in black velvet and diamonds, her short salt-and-pepper hair beautifully styled.

"Paula Romano," Paula responded. She turned to his father.

"Hello there, my dear. I'm Matthew Norman." His father's eyes were warmly admiring.

Matt wished he could disappear. Of all the things he didn't want to do, it was sit here and make pleasant conversation with his parents and Paula. But he smiled and promised himself he'd never allow himself to get in a situation like this one again. He watched his parents charm Paula. His mother, always at ease in any situation, seemed perfectly relaxed as she chatted brightly.

"And have you known Matt long?" Betty Norman asked. The question sounded innocent, but Matt knew the wheels were turning in his mother's head. She, too, wanted grandchildren—wanted Matt to marry. Were all parents like his?

"No. We . . . uh . . . sort of ran into each other a couple of days ago," Paula said with an impish smile, flashing those dimples once more.

"Oh?" Betty Norman's eyebrows rose.

Matt explained about the accident.

His mother smiled. "Well, dear," she said, turning to Paula, "he doesn't seem to have held it against you."

Matt sighed. He loved his mother, but sometimes he felt like strangling her. From earliest childhood, she'd seemed to delight in embarrassing him. She was always saying outlandish things, trying to manipulate him, just as she did his father. No wonder he'd moved out of the family home as soon as he could.

"He's very fond of his new car, you know," his mother's lightly teasing voice continued. "He won't even let people smoke inside it. He's very set in his ways." She picked up a Japanese silk cigarette bag, opened it, and extracted a Virginia Slim. "Do you smoke?" she asked Paula as Matt's father reached for her lighter and flicked it. She inhaled deeply.

"No," Paula said. "In fact, I'm always on my father's case about smoking."

"It's not the smoke in my car I object to so much as your smoking at all," Matt said, stung by her remark but gratified by Paula's answer.

"One must have some vices," his mother said mildly. "Unlike you, darling, the rest of us aren't perfect." She turned to Paula. "I feel I must warn you, my dear. Matt is quite adamant about certain things."

Then, with a wicked gleam in her eyes, she said sotto voce, "He thoroughly disapproves of me, you know."

Matt sighed again. The puzzling thing about his mother was her ability to make his well-thought-out decisions seem somehow stuffy. Even when he knew he was right about something, she made him feel stodgy. And she always had to have the last word.

"What do you think, Matt?" his father said.

"What? Sorry. I wasn't paying attention."

"We wondered if you were free Saturday night."

"Uh . . . well, yes, as far as I know."

"Good," his mother said. "Your father and I are having a small dinner party, and we wanted you to be there. You can bring Paula."

Matt opened his mouth, then closed it. She'd done it again. Bring Paula? He wasn't sure if he wanted to *see* Paula again. He wasn't sure about anything concerning Paula. "Really, Mother," he said in as calm a voice as he could muster. "It's presumptuous of us to think Paula has no plans for Saturday night or that she'd even want to come to a boring dinner party."

"Oh, it won't be boring, darling. It's in honor of the Garibaldis, and you know how much fun they are. The Whittakers and the Sebastians are coming, too. Even Rory," she added. "Paula will love it." She smiled as if everything was settled, patting Paula's hand.

Maybe strangling would be too easy a way to die. Maybe he should hang her by her perfectly manicured nails and torture her. He looked at Paula. Her big eyes were glowing, and an attractive flush stained her cheeks. "I'm looking forward to it," she said.

Matt knew when he was beaten. He'd deal with his mother later. For now he'd better get out of here before his mother decided to invite Paula to join them all on a cruise or something. Then, surprisingly, Paula solved his problem for him.

"It's been delightful meeting you, Mrs. Norman, Mr. Norman," she said. "But it's really getting late, and I have to be in early tomorrow. We'd better be going."

"What kind of work do you do, dear?" asked his mother.

"I work part-time for my father. He has a small pool supply and service business, and I help him with the books as well as answer service calls."

"Really?"

Paula made a disparaging gesture. "It's not what I want to do forever. I've got other interests, but this pays the bills."

"There's nothing wrong with what you're doing, my dear," said Betty. "Don't ever be ashamed of honest work. My own father worked in the steel mills all of his life, and I'm proud of it. He was a good man."

"Oh, I'm not ashamed of it," Paula said.

"I've never worked at anything," Betty said. "I met Matthew in college, we married, and I've never earned a dime of my own."

"The work you do is important, Betty," said Matt's father. He turned to Paula. "She does charity work. Lots of it, and everyone is grateful."

"My mother is a bleeding heart," Matt said. "I'll never forget the time I came home from school and found the entire house overrun with homeless families."

Betty Norman chuckled. "You should have seen the look on his face! I think I embarrassed him."

"Embarrassed me! I was mortified." He laughed, too. "It was a frigid January day, and Mother had taken in two families. It seemed like there were people everywhere—squalling kids, sad-faced women, hopeless-looking men. I couldn't believe it. They were sitting on the satin brocade sofa, sprawling on the Aubusson carpet, laying on the guest-room beds. Mother's favorite charity, a local shelter, had run out of room, and she just opened up the entire house. There were even two kids in my room!''

Matthew Norman joined in the muffled laughter, and Matt saw Paula's eyes twinkle at the spectacle Matt had painted.

''He wrinkled his nose up,'' Betty Norman said, ''and I yanked him into the kitchen and told him that he should never turn up his nose at poor, unfortunate people. He was an awful snob at that age.''

Matt picked up the story. ''She said just because they didn't have anything didn't mean they were lesser people. She said we were just lucky, that's all.''

''And she was right,'' Paula said. ''You know, Mrs. Norman, what you did sounds exactly like something I'd do.''

How had he known that? Matt wondered with a sinking heart.

''But I'd embarrass my mother! Not the other way around.'' Paula's laugh was joined by both senior Normans.

Matt could sympathize with Paula's mother. Although he had gotten over his childhood embarrassment, and even contributed heavily to many of his mother's charity interests, he knew he'd never feel entirely comfortable with her causes.

''I'm only working for my father until my real love pays off,'' Paula said, and Matt was grateful for the change of subject.

''Oh?'' Betty Norman's ears perked up. Matt winced.

They'd never get out of here. His mother had found a soul mate in Paula.

"I used to be an elementary-school music teacher, but I didn't like it. It left me no time to do what I really want to do."

"Which is?" his mother prompted.

"I write songs," Paula said proudly.

Matt saw his parents look at each other. He wondered what they were thinking. Betty Norman turned her attention back to Paula. "That's fascinating, my dear."

"I used to perform, too. In fact, I sang the National Anthem at an Oilers game last year."

Matt nearly choked. She'd said it as if she'd been invited to sing the lead in *Carmen* at the Met. He darted a quick glance at his parents, but they were both grinning at Paula. Amazing. "What kind of songs do you write?" he asked, fascinated in spite of himself. Although he'd never harbored any desire to do anything of the sort, there was a certain mystique about people who were involved in show business.

"I'm experimenting with country music . . . ballads, you know." Her dark eyes sparkled with eagerness. "I've been sending my stuff out, but so far, nothing's come of it. Right now I've got some material with Lindy Perkins."

"Lindy Perkins!" All three Normans said the name simultaneously. Lindy Perkins, the blond bombshell of country music, was big time. In spite of himself, Matt felt a tug of reluctant admiration for the guts evidenced by Paula.

"She'll probably reject them, but what the heck? If you never try, nothing will ever happen," Paula said.

"That's very true," his father said.

Matt stood up. "I think it's time to leave."

*   *   *

Matt was so quiet on the way home that Paula began to worry he was angry with her. After a few attempts to get him to talk, Paula gave up and stared out the window at the lights dotting the Katy Freeway. She loved Houston at night. The city reminded her of a giant surrealistic painting, brilliant and throbbing with life.

When they pulled up in front of her townhouse, Matt courteously walked around to open her door and reached for her hand. When she felt his strong, warm hand enveloping hers, a curious sensation tingled through her. As she stepped into the cool night air, she shivered.

"Let's get you inside. It's chilly out here," he said.

They walked to her front door, and she slowly turned to face him. "Would you like to come in for a drink?"

"No, thanks," he said. "You have to get up early, remember?"

Paula nodded, suddenly uncertain. His face was in shadow. She could smell the clean scent of his aftershave. Her heart beat a tiny bit faster. "Well, thank you for a lovely evening."

"My pleasure." His voice was polite but had a distant tone.

"Matt?"

"Yes?"

She could sense the rigidity in his body. "What's the matter?"

"Nothing."

"Are you angry because your parents invited me to their party Saturday night?"

"No."

Paula sighed. All her pleasure in the evening disappeared. He was unhappy, and that invitation from his mother was the only thing she could think of that would have made him so. Nothing else had happened. On the way home he'd probably had time to think about the entire situation, and now he was embarrassed and didn't know how to get out of it. Obviously, he didn't like her and didn't want to see her again. Maybe he was still a snob at heart.

Fine, she thought. *I'll make it easy for him. I'll make up some excuse and call him tomorrow and tell him I can't go. He's too mainstream for my taste anyway. Give me a musician with hang-ups any day.* "Good night, Matt," she said, touching his sleeve in farewell.

His arm jerked away from her as if she'd touched him with a hot poker. Paula shrank back against the door. Then, to her utter amazement, he pulled her into his arms.

The kiss was hot and wild. Paula could feel the blood pound through her body, and after the first shocked seconds, she raised her arms and twined them around his neck. She could feel every hard line of his body, the corded muscles straining and holding her so tightly. Her head whirled; he could certainly kiss!

Paula's mouth opened under his, and she kissed him back with enthusiasm. In answer, Matt's arms held her locked close, his lips and tongue hot and seeking. His hands stroked her bare back, spreading heat wherever they touched. Paula's insides felt like melted butter.

When they finally drew apart, both of them were breathing hard. Her knees were weak as his hand caressed her cheek, the palm smooth. She shuddered. *Wow*, she thought. *What have we here?*

His eyes glittered in the dark. "You're cold," he said, a husky edge to his voice.

"No, I'm not cold at all." Her voice sounded odd to her ears.

"Don't say anything, Paula," he murmured. He bent and brushed his lips against hers, whispering against her mouth as she opened it to answer. "Shh. Let's not spoil this. I'll call you Saturday." Then he turned away and strode swiftly down the walk.

Paula stared at his retreating back. Her thoughts churned. Shakily, she turned and unlocked her door, letting herself into the townhouse. Miss Milly raised her head from her curled-up position on the couch. Her green-flecked eyes studied Paula solemnly.

"Don't look at me like that," Paula said aloud. "I know I'm crazy. I know that I started all this to teach him a lesson. I know if I had any sense at all I'd never see him again."

The cat purred.

"My sentiments exactly," Paula said.

FOUR

Matt tried not to think about Paula or the events of the previous evening, but the more he tried to banish the memories from his mind, the more they refused to be banished.

Paula Romano. Even her name evoked images of dark, hot nights, perfumed tropical flowers, and lilting Gypsy music. And she had the strangest effect on him. When he was around her he found himself acting completely out of character, doing things he never intended to do.

Last night, for instance, when they'd been standing so close together on her front stoop, he certainly hadn't meant to kiss her. What he'd meant to do was give her a casual handshake, smile politely, and say good night. He started to do just that.

Then, when he leaned toward her, the scent of her filled him, scrambling his brains or something. And when she touched him, her dark eyes glowing in the navy night, something wild and fierce leaped inside him. Before he even realized what he was doing, he reached for her, yanking her up against him, and his mouth covered hers.

Matt closed his eyes, remembering the intoxicating taste of her warm, soft lips and her sweet mouth and tongue, the feel of her small, deliciously curved body that had fitted against him as perfectly as a connecting piece in a jigsaw puzzle. Her skin was smooth and silky, her hair fragrant and thick. He'd felt his control slipping. After all, a man could only take so much temptation. He mustered up all the willpower he possessed and dragged his mouth away from hers, stopping the kiss before it raged totally out of control. His body ached from the effort, and it took a long time for him to settle down afterward. Even now, he could feel the tightness in his belly, the desire aroused by thoughts of Paula and the kiss they'd shared.

Lord, he thought, *just what is it about that damned girl that has me so tied up in knots?* For two cents he'd call her tomorrow and make up some excuse—any excuse—for not taking her to his parents' dinner party. Because he liked his nice, orderly life and soothing routine. And he had a feeling letting Paula Romano into this calm existence would be tantamount to unleashing a tiger in a room full of tame kittens.

His intercom buzzed, and he forced himself to put his disturbing thoughts out of his mind. He pressed the connecting button. "Yes, Rachel?"

"Mr. Norman, Mr. Tobias is here."

"Already? I'll be out in a minute." Matt glanced at his watch. He couldn't believe it was three o'clock— time for Benjamin Tobias's appointment, but it was. It was disconcerting to realize he'd spent so much time thinking about Paula. He was at least two hours off his schedule; there were still four items on his checklist for this afternoon that he had not yet attended to.

He lined up his pen set and calendar and straightened the edge of his desk blotter. Then he stood up, smoothed his hair, and walked out to Rachel's office. Normally his secretary would bring clients into his office, but Benjamin Tobias wasn't just any client. He was one of the half dozen top clients of the firm, and Matt had only been assigned to him a few months earlier. Before that, Tobias had worked with Clancy Beska, the oldest partner in the firm, who had recently died of a heart attack.

Matt had been shocked when Oscar Claybourne, the managing partner, told him he would now be Tobias's attorney.

"Why?" he asked. "Wouldn't he rather deal with one of you? Won't he feel slighted that he's being given to a junior partner?"

"We've already talked to him about you," Claybourne said. "He seemed agreeable."

"But—"

"You can handle the work, Matt."

"I'm not worried about whether I can handle it; I'm just concerned that Benjamin Tobias won't like working with me—won't feel the same confidence in me he felt in Mr. Beska. You know how Tobias is, sir. He's pretty set in his ways."

Oscar Claybourne filled his water glass from the carafe sitting in one corner of his desk. "Matt, the other senior partners and I have talked the situation over. Don't take this the wrong way, but the main reason we decided to assign Tobias to you is because the two of you are so much alike."

"Alike!" Matt couldn't believe Oscar Claybourne had said that.

Claybourne shrugged. Matt wondered if his father had known about this. He hadn't mentioned it if he had.

And so it was settled. Matt didn't agree with the

assessment, but he knew it would be useless to argue. He supposed this was a compliment anyway, a measure of the confidence the senior partners had in him and his abilities. He promised Claybourne that he would do his best. How he handled Benjamin Tobias was very important—not only to the firm but to Matt's own future, and he wouldn't jeopardize that. No matter how unjust the comparison between him and Tobias had been.

Now, as he greeted the older man, he wondered what Tobias thought of him. So far they had had no problems, but there had also been no major legal hurdles for Matt to handle. Matt had a feeling Tobias was still testing him—biding his time to make a final judgment.

They shook hands, and Matt motioned Tobias into his office, following closely behind. Although Benjamin Tobias wasn't tall or even very big, his compact, muscular frame exuded power—a feat not easy for a small man to achieve.

After Tobias was seated in one of the soft leather armchairs in front of the desk, Matt walked around and sat in his swivel chair once more. This was another departure from his established practice of sitting in the other armchair—a ploy to put his clients at ease, to encourage them to open up to him. With Tobias, Matt felt he needed the psychological edge of the desk between them.

He picked up the file on Tobias's company. "I was surprised when you called for an appointment, Ben . . ." he began.

"You can put that file down," Tobias said. His sharp, dark eyes under craggy brows missed nothing. "I didn't come today to talk about anything to do with Tobias Industries."

Matt waited, having long ago learned the advantage of keeping quiet and letting the other person talk.

"Indirectly, I suppose this does have something to do with business, but it's not anything you're going to find in that file." He fingered his tie, a maroon silk with gray stripes.

He seemed edgy, and that really surprised Matt. He'd never seen Benjamin Tobias anything other than completely confident, sure he was right about everything, and not afraid to tell you so. In fact, the trait about Tobias that Matt disliked most was his propensity toward pontification. That, and his rigidness. He guessed that's why it rankled so much that he should be compared to Tobias.

"I want to make a completely new will," Tobias said.

"Oh?" Matt hoped his face didn't give away his surprise. He knew for a fact that Tobias's current will had taken weeks to streamline.

"I want to change my main beneficiary," Tobias continued.

"Oh?" Matt said again, knowing he must sound stupid, but more than surprised now. In fact, he was shocked. Benjamin Tobias doted on his only child, David, who was currently the main beneficiary of the existing will.

Tobias's eyes narrowed. "If this doesn't work, nothing will."

The man was talking in riddles. "I'm not sure I understand," Matt said.

"It's simple. My son is making an ass of himself over some showgirl. He won't listen to a thing I say. I figure the girl's after his money—you know these show-business types, so if she finds out I've cut David out of my will, she'll drop him like a hot potato."

Matt studied the stiff posture, the clenched jaw, the determination in the steely gray eyes. Everything about Benjamin Tobias proclaimed he had made his decision and would brook no disagreement. Matt knew he should try to present any arguments for the other side, any reasons why Tobias might like to rethink his decision, but Matt actually agreed with Tobias's reasoning. Cutting David out of the will was a shrewd move. If the girl really loved David and cared nothing for the money, she'd marry him anyway, and Tobias could always change his will back to the original version. But if she didn't love David and was only interested in the money, Tobias would have averted a real mess. "Is David serious about her?" Matt asked.

"Yes. That's what pushed me to this point. When he first met her, I didn't worry too much. I thought he was just sowing a few wild oats, that this . . . this . . . infatuation would pass. But instead, he seems to have become totally besotted with her. Now he's talking about marrying her!"

"Maybe she's not as bad as you think," Matt temporized. "Have you met her?"

"I have no desire to meet her. I know the type. She's a singer, for God's sake. Sings in some dive in the Montrose area."

The way he said "Montrose area" almost made Matt smile. It was true that some parts of Montrose were seedy, but there were other parts that were trendy and upscale. However, Matt knew Tobias wouldn't thank him for pointing that out.

"And she hasn't got a good track record, either," Tobias added. "She's already got one failed marriage behind her. As far as I'm concerned, marriage should be forever."

Matt winced. "Sometimes things happen—"

"Things happen because people take the easy way out! Why, my Emily and I were married for nearly forty years, and lots of things happened, but we didn't quit!"

Matt knew it would be useless to say anything. He would never change the older man's mind.

"If that's what he wants . . . to *consort* with musicians, be a part of that whole loose-living lifestyle—divorce, drugs, alcohol, who knows what—well, that's his choice. But I don't have to aid and abet him." Tobias snorted. "And I sure as hell don't intend to!"

Matt suddenly thought of Paula. She was a musician. She'd said she had sung in clubs and at parties and now she was writing music. He wondered what Tobias would think about her. He'd probably class her in the same category as the luckless girl his son fancied. Matt squirmed. Tobias would probably lose all faith in him if he knew Matt was "consorting" with a singer himself. The old-fashioned word amused Matt, but he knew he'd better not let Tobias see that. He would resent any sign of levity, any indication that Matt didn't take this situation seriously. The man was a throwback to an earlier time with his strict ideas, but he was sincere about wanting the best for his son, Matt knew. Just like Matt's own parents wanted the best for him and his sister. Matt figured he'd be the same way with his children someday.

"Well, we'd better get started," he said, turning his full attention to his client.

One of the things Paula really appreciated about her job was that no matter how busy she was, she always had time to think. Time to think was a necessity when you were trying to write a song. Time to think was an impossibility when you were closeted in a classroom with twenty-some noisy children.

So the day after her dinner with Matt, even though she was swamped with work, she still had plenty of time to daydream about the previous evening. She sighed as she cleaned out a clogged, nasty-looking filter. Part of her mind was wondering why anyone who could afford to build a beautiful pool like this one would be so neglectful of simple maintenance; the other part of her mind lingered over the kiss she'd shared with Matt.

His giving her a good-night kiss wasn't, in itself, so surprising. After all, she wasn't a dog or anything! But the kiss itself had just about knocked her for a loop. She smiled, remembering how she'd felt when his mouth claimed hers. How her heart had pounded, how her head had spun. No doubt about it. The kiss had been a scorcher, sending fire through her body in a sizzling streak. Who'd have thought that the impeccable, controlled Matt Norman would be capable of a thousand-megawatt kiss?

She could feel her smile expand to a grin. That kiss had given her a glimpse at the inner Matt Norman, the one he took such trouble to hide. Matt might look cool on the surface, but underneath beat the heart of a hot-blooded man. She wondered what other surprises were in store for her. She could hardly wait for Saturday to come.

But before Saturday, she had a whole day to get through. And she had two regular weekly service calls to make before the day was over. One of the service calls was to her favorite customer, an older man she'd tagged Mr. T. because of his tough facade. She smiled with pleasure at the thought of the old curmudgeon, which was always how she thought of him. The time she spent talking to Mr. T. usually turned out to be the highlight of her working week.

She'd figured him out early on. Although she was sure he really was tough in his business dealings, underneath he was an old softie, no matter how he tried to hide it. When her father had first asked her to take over the account, Mr. T. hadn't liked it. She knew it, for he'd been stern and disapproving when she'd shown up that first day. He frowned forbiddingly, and she was sure he would call her father and ask for someone else.

"Hmmph, what's a girl doing grubbing around with pools?" he asked.

"It's honest work," Paula answered. She gave him her best smile as she checked the chlorine level in the pool.

He glowered down at her, his sharp eyes watching carefully.

Just waiting for me to make a mistake, she thought as she quietly and competently tested the acidity and alkalinity of the water, then added acid to bring it to the proper levels.

"Girl like you should be teaching school or working in an office," he said.

"I used to teach school," Paula said as she removed the filter, then walked to the outside faucet and began cleaning it. "I hated being inside all day long." She took a deep breath and looked up at the cornflower sky. Wisps of clouds floated by. "I love it out here. If God had intended us to stay indoors all day long, why did he make the outdoors so beautiful?" She turned to him then, grinning.

After one startled look, an answering smile spread over his face, making him look ten years younger.

That was the beginning of their friendship. From that day on, he had always been waiting for her when she arrived on Friday afternoons, and he usually followed her around, watching her as she worked. And they talked. At first they only talked about her work, or the weather, or his garden—which was his special joy. But lately, he'd been letting a little of his guard down and had begun to tell her about his wife who had died five years earlier, and his son. Paula always looked forward to their talks, for even though Mr. T. was unbending when it came to his ideas of morality and the way people should behave, he had begun to reveal more and more of that softer, inner self, and Paula was drawn to him. And, if she were honest, she enjoyed chipping away at his comfortable ideas; she'd even tried to shock him on occasion. Of course, he always knew she was baiting him, but he seemed to enjoy their friendly skirmishes, too. So it was with a pleasant tingle of anticipation that Paula headed toward West University.

But when she arrived at Mr. T.'s beautiful West U home, Regina, his housekeeper, told her Mr. T. wouldn't be there this week.

"Had an appointment downtown," Regina explained. "Kind of an emergency, I think, 'cause his face looked like thunder when he left."

Although disappointed, Paula knew the older man's absence was a blessing in disguise. She'd miss their weekly chat while she went about her work, but she'd get through so much faster, which meant she'd get home early tonight.

She had an idea for a new song, and she couldn't wait to work on it. A song called "Hot Kisses." Plus she was dying to phone Kim to tell her about her date with Matt and the upcoming dinner party. Maybe between the two of them they could figure out what she should wear.

*   *   *

"You're not working late again, are you?"

Matt looked up. Rory lounged in the doorway of the office. "I have to. I got way behind today. I should be caught up by seven, though."

"Man, it's Friday night. You know, T.G.I.F. Time to get down and par-teeee . . ." Rory held his arms as if there were a woman in them and danced into the room. "Come on, buddy-boy. Let's go out and howl. Put the damned work away. It'll keep until Monday. Let's go hit a few happy hours and meet a few chicks."

Matt shook his head. "Not tonight, Rory. I told you. I'm behind schedule."

Rory rolled his eyes. "Schedule! Schedule! Honestly, Matt, you act like you're an old man!"

"I don't feel like going out tonight."

Now Rory sighed theatrically. "I'm gonna have to find me a new best friend if you don't shape up. I can't count on you anymore. You're getting boring. You're way too young to be boring."

"I was out late last night, and I'm bushed," Matt said patiently, refusing to allow Rory to make him feel guilty. Rory was a party animal. Matt wasn't. Sometimes he enjoyed letting his hair down with Rory. But lately, he'd wanted to party less and less. He smiled ruefully. Maybe Rory was partially right. Maybe he *was* getting boring. Or maybe he was just bored with the things they had done for years. Maybe he was ready for a different kind of life.

"What about tomorrow night? You going to your parents' dinner party?" Rory plopped into one of the chairs in front of Matt's desk.

Matt sighed. "Yes, unfortunately."

Rory raised his eyebrows. "I thought you enjoyed that kind of thing. You always act like you do."

"Normally, I do. But tomorrow night I've been coerced into bringing someone I have no desire to bring."

"Anyone I know?" Rory slumped lower in the chair and propped his feet on the edge of Matt's desk.

Matt stiffened. He hated it when anyone did that, and Rory knew it. Matt wondered if his friend was purposely trying to irritate him. "That girl—the one who caused me to wreck my BMW."

"Oh?" An amused smile tugged at Rory's lips. "How'd that come about? I thought you said she wasn't your type. I thought you were never going to see her again."

Matt didn't like the look in Rory's eyes. "I wasn't. It just happened."

"Things like that don't just *happen*."

"Well . . ." Matt stalled, wishing Rory would leave but knowing there wasn't much chance of it.

"Well, what? Don't keep me in suspense. I can't wait to hear how this girl you never planned to see again just happens to be your date to a dinner party at your *parents'* house, of all places."

Since Matt knew Rory would never leave until he'd heard the entire story, he told him everything that had happened since they'd last discussed Paula. He explained about her bringing dinner to his house, about how he had apologized by sending her flowers, and about last night's events.

"She certainly has guts," Rory said admiringly. The smile that had begun earlier seemed a permanent part of his face as he grinned at Matt. "I sure would have liked to have seen your face when she showed up on your doorstep!" Then he laughed out loud. "And Jill! I can't imagine the ice princess's reaction!"

Rory was the only one in the office who knew about

Matt dating Jill, and he had always called her the ice princess because he said she reminded him of Grace Kelly. But Matt thought Rory had probably tried to date her with no success.

"It wasn't funny." Matt eyed the files on his desk longingly. He wished he'd never gotten started with this conversation. "I had to send her flowers, too."

"So is she speaking to you again?"

"She thanked me for the flowers."

Rory grinned. "That's better than nothing. But let's get back to this Paula. I can't wait to meet her. She sounds like the kind of girl I'd like."

"Too bad she didn't wreck your car, then," Matt grumbled.

A devilish glint appeared in Rory's dark eyes. "If you're not interested in her, maybe you'd like to let me have a chance with her," he drawled. "Unless, of course, you're just *saying* you're not . . ." He paused. ". . . when you really are."

"Hell, no, I'm not just *saying* it! Feel perfectly free to make your move. I'll introduce you to her tomorrow night." Sometimes Rory gave him a royal pain. "So now that we've settled that, do you think you could remove your feet from my desk and let me get back to work?"

That infuriating smile was still firmly in place. "Okay. Whatever you say." Rory swung his long legs off the desk, stood up, and buttoned his suit jacket. "Sure you won't change your mind about tonight?"

"I told you. I'm tired." *And I'm getting damned tired of you.* Matt picked up the Tobias will. He wanted to read it through thoroughly before he left tonight.

"All right," Rory drawled again. He turned to leave, then stopped. His voice was tinged with laughter. "But don't forget. Just give me the high sign tomorrow night,

and if I like this Paula, I'll take her off your hands."
He chuckled.

"Don't slam the door on your way out," Matt said.

On Saturday Paula spent two hours trying on everything in her closet. A small dinner party. That's how Betty Norman had described it. And Paula knew the elder Normans lived in River Oaks. So the dinner party would probably be elegant and dressy, but surely not formal or Betty Norman would have said something.

Although Paula prided herself on being a nonconformist, she was female enough to love dressing up.

At the end of the two hours, she still hadn't found anything suitable, even though clothing lay in discarded heaps all over her room. She looked at her watch. It was only four o'clock, and when Matt had called her earlier, he'd said he'd pick her up at seven. There was just enough time.

Thirty minutes later Paula dashed into Alaina's, her favorite boutique. "I need something really smashing to wear to a dinner party in River Oaks," she explained to the tall woman with spiked hair who owned the shop. "And hang the cost," Paula added recklessly. She shoved the mental image of the already-high balance on her MasterCard out of her mind.

So at a quarter of seven, as Paula put the finishing touches to her makeup, fluffed up her hair and gave it a good spray, and finally stepped back to study herself in her full-length mirror, she was satisfied.

The dress was exactly right, she thought. Perfect, in fact. When Alaina produced it, a smile curving her mouth, Paula knew immediately it was the sort of dress she wanted. Made of clinging black crepe, the front had a high neckline with a mandarin collar. Except for the band around her neck, the back of the dress was bare to the waist. The skirt was long and straight, slit to midthigh on one side. Paula smiled at her reflection in the mirror. Yes. The dress was perfect. Even if it *had* cost most of a week's salary. With it she wore her gold bangle bracelet and a thick gold necklace her parents had given her for her twenty-fifth birthday. Long gold earrings completed the ensemble.

When the doorbell rang at exactly seven, Paula moved unhurriedly to answer it. A glow of satisfaction filled her as she saw Matt's eyes widen, and she knew in that moment the dress had been worth every penny she'd spent on it.

Matt hated the dress. It was long and black and shifted suggestively against her body each time she moved; it was a dress calculated to arouse a man. A knot of heat formed in his stomach as he stared at her.

He finally found his tongue and said, "Ready?"

She nodded and picked up a short velvet jacket that was laying on a small cherrywood table in the foyer, and as she turned Matt saw the flash of long leg exposed by the slit in her skirt. He also saw that the dress was entirely backless, and he sucked in his breath. He had a sudden image of Rory's laughing face when he'd said, "If *I* like her, I'll take her off your hands."

"Darn cat," she muttered as she brushed at the jacket. "I'd like to kill her! There're cat hairs all over this jacket."

"Cat?" Matt said, forgetting the dress, forgetting Rory. He backed up two steps. He hated cats.

Paula glanced up. "What's wrong?"

"I can't stand cats."

"If I were you I wouldn't say that quite so loud.

Miss Milly is very sensitive. If she hears you saying you hate her, she'll make your life miserable."

The words were no sooner out of Paula's mouth than a huge calico poked her face around the corner. The cat stared, the fur on her back and her long tail bristling. Her green eyes fastened on his. She hissed.

"Too late," Paula murmured. "I think she heard you."

Matt eyed the cat warily. "You don't really believe she understands what we're saying." *Miss Milly. What an idiotic name.*

"Of course she understands. But never mind. I'll smooth her ruffled feelings later."

He should have known. He opened his mouth to say something, then closed it again. What good would it do? He knew other cat people. In fact, his sister was one of them. They were totally irrational when it came to the subject of cats, whether theirs or someone else's.

The calico continued to stare at him with an unblinking, unnerving gaze.

Matt stared back. Even being this close to the feline gave him the creeps. Sly, sneaky things.

As he and Paula walked out the door, the cat hissed again.

"Don't worry," Paula said. "After you've been here a few times, she'll be friendly."

He frowned. *After he'd been here a few times?* Did she think this was the start of a relationship? The only reason he was taking her out tonight was because his mother had manuevered him into it. He had no intention of ever seeing that cat again.

"What are you? A dog person?" Paula asked once they were in the car and on their way to his parents' home.

Matt shifted gears as he rounded one of the many S-curves on Memorial Drive. "Not really. I'm just not crazy about animals, period." He resolutely pushed aside the memory of a small mongrel puppy who had followed him home from school one day. He'd named her Shadow because she always seemed to be two steps behind him. He and Shadow were inseparable for ten months. Then, one day while he was at school, she got out of the gate when the gardener carelessly left it open.

She was hit by a car. She died at the vet's office that afternoon. His mother was waiting for him when he got home from school, her eyes full of pity.

He'd never wanted another pet.

"You don't like *any* animals?" Paula said. She sounded incredulous.

"They're not worth the trouble. Lots of people feel the way I do." In fact, Matt thought, an aversion to animals was sensible. Much more sensible than allowing them to take over your life—setting you up for disappointment—and your home, where they were likely to leave hair everywhere, not to mention fleas in the carpets, and all kinds of other messes. Above all else, Matt hated messes.

He expected Paula to argue with him, but oddly, she didn't. She was silent the rest of the way to his parents' house, and once or twice Matt sneaked a look at her and wondered what she was thinking. Maybe she was worried about the dinner party. He wondered what his parents' friends would think of her. She was certainly different from Sarah.

Matt turned onto the winding, tree-lined street where his parents lived. "We're almost there," he said.

A few minutes later the house came into view. Matt had always loved the house—an enormous brick two-story Colonial with graceful white pillars across the front and a long, curving driveway. Its traditional design, serene setting, and understated elegance had always transmitted a sense of peace and calm. Tonight the house blazed with light, both inside and outside, and a half-dozen cars lined the drive. Matt recognized Rory's red Corvette and the elder Sebastians' white Lincoln.

As Matt helped Paula out of the car, the spicy fragrance of her perfume floated around him, mingling with the cool breeze. She tilted her head up and smiled, dimples flashing.

"Why didn't you tell me your parents lived in Tara?"

"I beg your pardon?"

Laughter bubbled from her mouth. "You know . . . Tara. From *Gone with the Wind*. That's what this house reminds me of."

Matt couldn't decide if she was making fun of the house. They walked together up the drive, up the four broad steps, and onto the stone veranda. Matt rang the bell. Within moments the huge double doors opened, and Phyllis, his mother's longtime maid, ushered them in.

"Matt, there you are," his mother said as she walked into the foyer. She beamed at Paula. "Hello, my dear. How lovely you look. What a beautiful dress."

"Thank you," Paula said.

Matt could tell she was pleased. He wondered if his mother really liked the dress or was just trying to put Paula at ease. His mother wore a long red silk tube dress with her ruby-and-diamond earrings, an anniversary present from his father. She looked perfect, as always. Smiling, she took Paula's arm, leading her toward the huge rectangular-shaped living room to the left of the foyer. Matt followed along behind.

His mother started introducing Paula to the other

guests, who stood chatting as they sipped their drinks. Matt waved to Rory who stood at the far end of the room, one arm propped on the mantel over the fire- place. Rory winked but made no move toward him, so Matt joined the group his mother had taken Paula to, which consisted of all the older men—Matt's father, Rory's father, Phillip Sebastian, Gino Garibaldi, one of his father's oldest friends and one of the richest men in Houston, and Simon Whittaker, another old friend. These four men had played golf together every Friday afternoon since Matt could remember. Matt watched as they studied Paula. Simon Whittaker seemed particu- larly interested. Matt knew that Simon, like his father, had hoped that Matt and Sarah, Simon's only daughter, would eventually marry.

When his mother led Paula toward the women, Matt excused himself and went with them. He was curious to see the females' reaction to Paula.

"I'd like you to meet Matt's friend, Paula Romano," his mother said as they approached. She named the women one by one. "Carolyn Whittaker, and this is her daughter, Sarah; Joanna Sebastian—she's Phillip's wife and Rory's mother. Have you met Rory? No? Well, you will. He's over there." His mother gestured in Rory's direction. "And this is Lucia Garibaldi and her daughter, Tessa. Her son is talking to Rory."

"How nice to meet you," said Joanna Sebastian, a tall, slender woman with a narrow, lively face.

"What a stunning dress," said Sarah Whittaker, giv- ing Matt a conspiratorial wink.

Matt grinned. Sarah was one of the nicest people he knew. It really *was* a shame they weren't attracted to each other, because she'd make the perfect wife. She looked particularly attractive tonight, with her straight, shining blond hair pulled back from her heart-shaped face, and the pale-blue chiffon of her demure cocktail dress picking up the blue of her eyes. He'd never known her to wear the wrong thing, say the wrong thing, or do the wrong thing.

"Romano? Are you Italian, then?" asked Lucia Garibaldi, her topaz eyes glittering with interest.

"Yes, I am," Paula said. Although her head was swimming from all the names, she had no trouble remembering Lucia's.

"Gino! Did you hear that? Italian!" She punctuated her words with expressive hand gestures, and the motion caused the many rings on her fingers to catch the light.

Paula liked the way she pronounced it—*EE-talian*. Tessa, a smaller version of her topaz-eyed, dark-haired mother, said, "Your name seems familiar. Do you belong to the club?"

Paula shook her head no. Although she had no idea to what club Tessa was referring, it really didn't matter, because Paula didn't belong to any clubs.

"What does your father do?" Lucia asked. "We probably know him. We know all the Italians in Houston."

"He owns a pool-service and supply company," Paula said, inwardly amused at Lucia's statement. What Lucia hadn't said, but Paula understood perfectly, was that the Garibaldis knew all the wealthy Italians in Houston.

"Oh." Lucia Garibaldi frowned. "I don't think I've heard of it."

"Well, there are a lot of pool-service companies. You couldn't be expected to know them all. We're located in Alief."

"Alief?"

Paula suppressed a smile. The way Lucia Garibaldi

said *Alief*, you'd have thought Paula had said Afghanistan. Well, she supposed if you were a part of the River Oaks crowd, Alief might seem as remote as a foreign country. She shrugged. "My family lives in Alief; they always have."

"If you'll excuse us, I'm going to drag Paula away for a minute and introduce her to Rory and Giovanni," Matt said.

He took her elbow, and Paula felt a zing of pleasure at the warm contact. "You don't have to rescue me, Matt," she said as they walked away.

"I wasn't rescuing you! I thought you'd probably like to meet these guys."

Although he'd denied her assertion, Paula saw the telltale blush he couldn't control. That was sweet, she thought. Although she hadn't been uncomfortable with the questions Lucia Garibaldi had asked, it was considerate of Matt to think of her feelings.

"This is my oldest friend, Rory Sebastian," Matt said as they approached the two men who were in animated conversation at the far end of the room. "And this Romeo is Giovanni Garibaldi, who's been breaking hearts all over the world ever since he turned fifteen."

Paula immediately liked Rory Sebastian. His dark, lively eyes and narrow face were sharp and clever and filled with amusement. She wasn't sure about Giovanni Garibaldi, though. Slickly handsome, he was almost too sure of himself as he took her hand and raised it to his lips with practiced charm.

"Beautiful," he murmured. "Matt, you've outdone yourself this time." He gave her a lingering look, his eyes sweeping her from head to toe.

So he was transparent. So what? As long as she didn't take him seriously, she might as well have fun.

"Thank you," she murmured, giving him her most brilliant smile. Then she turned to Rory Sebastian.

"So this is Paula," he drawled. "I've been looking forward to meeting you."

Not able to keep the surprise out of her voice, she said, "Well, I see my fame has spread. Has Matt been talking about me?"

Matt's laugh sounded a bit self-conscious. "I told Rory how we met."

Rory grinned and winked. "You, pretty girl, can run into me any old time you like."

Paula laughed. "You might not say so if you could see Matt's car."

"What's a car compared to the opportunity to meet you?"

"That's what I tried to tell him, but he didn't seem to appreciate it at the time."

"Matt takes everything too seriously." Rory poked Matt in the ribs. "I'm always telling him to loosen up."

"And you take things too lightly," Matt said, but Paula thought she heard a note of strain—or was it irritation?—in his voice.

"The one thing I *don't* take lightly is the chance to spend time with a beautiful girl," Rory retorted, eyes twinkling. "How about you, Giovanni?"

"Absolutely not." Giovanni gave Paula a little half-bow. "I see you have no champagne, Paula. Would you like me to get you a glass? And when I return, someone must please explain to me about this car. Obviously there is some story here of which I am not aware."

"All right," she said.

"Well, since it looks as if you're in good hands,"

Matt said, "I'm going over to talk to Phillip Sebastian for a while."

He walked away before Paula could respond. She wondered if he were angry with her. Or—the thought hit her suddenly—maybe he was jealous! She supposed she had been flirting with his friends. A warm surge of satisfaction crept over her. If Matt wasn't interested in her, he wouldn't be jealous.

For the next fifteen minutes, she gave her full attention to Rory Sebastian and Giovanni Garibaldi, who were flatteringly attentive. Rory, in particular, was fun to be around. Giovanni she could take or leave. But since she had decided to fan Matt's jealousy a bit—if it *was* jealousy—Giovanni suited her purposes just fine. She wasn't sure if she was succeeding, though, because when she sneaked a look in Matt's direction, he had his back to her and was in earnest conversation with Phillip Sebastian. Then the next time she looked, Matt and Sarah Whittaker had their heads together and were talking. Paula frowned, turned to Giovanni and Rory, and redoubled her efforts to be amusing.

When Betty Norman announced dinner, Rory insisted on taking her into the dining room.

"But maybe Matt . . ." she started to say.

"Forget Matt," Rory said. "I'm a heck of a lot more fun." He smiled down at her. "Now, where were we?"

FIVE

Betty Norman had placed Paula in the middle of the table between Simon Whittaker and Rory.

"Isn't *this* lucky?" Rory whispered in her ear as he held her chair for her. "I get to sit next to the best-looking girl in the room."

What a line! Paula thought, even as she smiled at Rory. She reached for her napkin and saw that Matt was directly across the table from her, and the blonde—Sarah—was sitting next to him. He'd been watching her and Rory, she could tell. For a minute she felt uncomfortable, and that made her angry. She hadn't done anything wrong. What was she supposed to do? Sit here like a bump on a log, doing nothing? After all, Matt wasn't paying any attention to her. She gave him her sweetest smile. He pretended he didn't see it and turned to say something to Sarah.

Paula turned to Rory. Two could play this game. But why was Rory so willing to play it? He really had been flirting with her outrageously, and if he was such a good friend of Matt's, why would he do that? It was almost as if he were doing it on purpose.

No, that was ridiculous. Rory was flirting with her because that was his nature. So she might as well relax and enjoy it. And if Matt was jealous, well, that was *his* problem. It would do him good to see that she was desirable in Rory's eyes.

As soon as everyone was seated, a uniformed waiter appeared and began pouring wine into the smaller of the wineglasses at each place. Paula glanced down at her place setting. She shook her head and laughed to herself. River Oaks or not, her own mother set a more formal table when she entertained.

"What're you so amused about?" Rory asked.

"My mother usually has at least eight pieces of silver on the table even when she's only having the family for dinner," Paula explained. "I guess I expected the same sort of thing here."

"Your mother must do some fancy entertaining."

"Not really. She just wanted all of us kids to know what fork to use when we went out in company."

"My mother had more serious things to worry about when she sent *me* out in company," Rory declared. "Isn't that right, Ma?"

Joanna Sebastian, who sat on Matt's other side, grimaced. "If you don't pay any attention to him, Paula, he might stop acting like an idiot. He likes an audience."

"Not just *any* audience," Rory said. He twirled an imaginary mustache, then said in a perfect imitation of Count Dracula, "I prefer ze voluptuous, dark-haired beauties. Ze blood is sweeterrrr . . ." He leaned toward Paula and pretended to take a bite out of her arm.

Paula giggled. He was such a fool. Across the table Sarah laughed, too, but Matt looked disgusted and scowled at Rory.

Throughout dinner, Rory kept up a running commentary of wicked remarks. Paula couldn't help laughing at him. He was thoroughly and completely irreverent, but in a nice way. She knew instinctively that Rory didn't have a mean bone in his body—only a well-developed sense of the ridiculous. She also knew he didn't take himself or anyone else too seriously. It struck her that he and Matt were an odd pair to be such good friends. Matt seemed to take everything seriously.

Each time Rory made an outrageous remark, Paula glanced at Matt. Once or twice she caught him looking at her, but most of the time he'd be talking and laughing with Sarah. A funny feeling settled into her stomach, then she got mad at herself. Just because he was ignoring her didn't mean he wasn't completely aware of her across the table.

But as she watched them, she couldn't help realizing that Matt and Sarah Whittaker *were* perfectly suited to each other. Looking at them together . . . they could have come from the same pea pod, they were so alike. Both healthy-looking blondes, both the product of private schools and old-line families, both on the quiet, well-bred side—they were like a matched pair of Thoroughbred horses.

Sarah would make Matt an ideal wife, Paula thought, trying to ignore the sudden emptiness she felt. Then she got angry with herself. It was crazy to be bothered by the thought that Matt and Sarah Whittaker were so compatible and that Matt obviously liked Sarah so much. *After all*, Paula told herself, *you have no interest in marriage. So why should you resent someone like Sarah?*

But even as she told herself this, she couldn't stop from wondering if Matt had ever given Sarah a kiss filled with the same fierce demand as the one he'd given her. The thought caused a knot to form in her chest, and she forced it from her mind.

Suddenly Paula wished she hadn't come tonight. Nothing about the evening had turned out the way she'd imagined it would.

Finally dessert was served, and Rory gave his attention to Tessa Garibaldi, seated on his other side. Paula turned to Simon Whittaker.

"So how did you and Matthew meet?" he asked, his shrewd gray eyes appraising.

Paula told him.

"I see. I *had* wondered. You're not from around here, are you?"

"I've lived in Houston all my life," Paula said, not completely sure what Whittaker had meant by his remark.

Whittaker gave her a sharp glance. "What I meant was, you don't live in this area. I know just about all of Sarah and Matthew's friends." He gave a fond glance to the pair across the table. "They've known each other since they were toddlers, you know."

Paula decided to ignore his last remark. "I grew up on the southwest side—the Alief area."

"I'm not familiar with that part of Houston," he said. "Do you live with your parents?"

"Not any longer. I own a townhouse off the Katy Freeway."

"And what do you do for a living, my dear?"

Paula wasn't fooled by the "my dear." Simon Whittaker didn't like her. She could see it in his eyes. And she thought she had a pretty good idea why.

"I work for my father."

"Oh? Doing what?"

"He has a pool-service and supply business." Before

Whittaker could phrase his next question, Paula said, "I help him with the books, and I answer service calls."

She could almost see the wheels turning in Whittaker's head as he assessed her answer and pondered his next question. Stuffy old goat, she thought. Although to be fair, he was probably only trying to protect Sarah's interests. He couldn't know Paula had no permanent designs on Matt. Or anyone, for that matter.

"How interesting," he finally said. "And do you *like* this type of work?"

"What Paula failed to tell you is that she has a master's degree in music but hated teaching," Matt interjected. "That's when she went to work for her father."

Paula didn't know whether to be annoyed with Matt for thinking she needed defending—after all, there was nothing wrong with what she did for a living—or flattered that he cared enough about her feelings to defend her to Sarah's father.

"You hated teaching?" Tessa Garibaldi asked. "Why?"

Now all conversation had ceased and everyone's attention was trained on Paula.

"I didn't like being cooped up all day long," she explained. "Plus, it wasn't really what I wanted to do with my life."

"And servicing swimming pools *is?*" Whittaker asked, his tone of voice clearly stating what he thought of the profession.

"Oh, for heaven's sakes, Simon," Carolyn Whittaker said. "You sound like such a snob."

"I only meant that I can't imagine a young woman of Paula's obvious intelligence aspiring to service swimming pools," Whittaker said, not in the least ruffled by his wife's reprimand.

I'll bet that's what you meant. "No, servicing swimming pools *isn't* what I aspire to do with my life,'' Paula answered coolly. She decided she didn't need rescuing by Sarah's mother, either. ''My real love is still music; I just didn't want to teach. I'm a composer.''

''Really?'' Tessa squealed. ''How fascinating! What kind of music?''

''Country western and pop, mostly.''

''That's a pretty tough business,'' Rory said, serious for once that evening. ''Had any luck?''

''No,'' Paula admitted. ''I've been sending my stuff off for a couple of years now, but so far, no one has been interested. But I have no intention of giving up.''

By now the dessert dishes were being cleared, and soon the talk went in other directions. When dinner was over, though, Sarah Whittaker came up to Paula and reintroduced the topic. Her light-blue eyes were friendly as she said, ''Paula, I'm so jealous of you. I've always harbored a secret desire to act, but I never had the nerve to do anything about it. Tell me what progress you've made.''

So Paula told her about the songs she'd sent to Lindy Perkins. ''I hope to hear from her soon. It's been weeks since I sent the tape.''

''I'll keep my fingers crossed for you. Please let me know the outcome.''

She seemed really interested, and Paula, despite her misgivings over Sarah's relationship with Matt, found herself liking the other woman.

''Maybe we could have lunch together soon,'' Sarah suggested.

''I'd like that,'' Paula said, and meant it.

People began saying their good-byes. Sarah rejoined her parents, and finally Matt walked toward Paula.

''Ready to leave?'' he asked.

"If you are."

He nodded. "Let's go say good-bye to the others."

They made the rounds, and when they got to Rory, Rory clasped Matt around the shoulders and said, "This girl's dynamite, Matt." He winked at her.

Paula smiled, but it took an effort. She could see by the cold expression in Matt's eyes that he wasn't amused by Rory's attentions to her, and she was afraid he might have been pushed too far.

But Rory either didn't see Matt's reaction or chose to ignore it, for he continued. "Too bad we're such good friends, or I'd be giving you a run for your money with Paula."

"It's a free country," Matt said stiffly.

Paula's heart sank. What had seemed so entertaining earlier in the evening had suddenly become stale. "Good-bye, Rory," she said, extending her hand, trying to keep her own voice casual. "It was nice meeting you."

"I'm looking forward to seeing you again soon," Rory said. Then he winked. His dark eyes glinted with suppressed amusement, and Paula knew for certain that he was purposely goading Matt. What she couldn't figure out was why.

Matt took her arm and steered her toward his parents.

"Please come again, my dear," Betty Norman said.

"Yes, we'd love to see you again," Matt's father said. He smiled, and although the smile was warm, Paula thought he looked very tired.

"Thank you," Paula said. Matt stood quietly. He didn't echo the invitation.

He was silent and remote as they pulled out of the driveway. Paula stared out the window as they drove west on San Felipe toward the Loop. With each mile that ticked away, her spirits sank lower. Although getting Matt to ask her out had started as a lark—a challenge that intrigued her—her feelings had changed subtly after last night. Unfortunately, their relationship seemed to have deteriorated this evening, and now she wasn't sure what she should do.

"Did you enjoy yourself tonight?"

The question startled her with its abruptness.

"Yes, I did." She looked at Matt, but he was staring straight ahead, his profile etched in sharp relief. "Your friends are very nice."

"You're a fast worker, aren't you?"

Paula's heart skittered at the unmistakable sound of anger in his voice. "What exactly does that remark mean?"

"I think you know." His teeth sounded as if they were clenched together. The car shot forward as he accelerated up the entrance ramp and joined the fast-moving traffic on the Loop.

"Spell it out for me," she said. Her own anger simmered beneath the surface. *He has his nerve. Ignore me all night, then act like a horse's ass because I talked to Rory.* She conveniently pushed aside the knowledge that Matt had come to her defense quickly when he thought she needed help.

"Oh, I think you can figure it out!"

Paula felt like smacking him. And if he hadn't been driving a car, she would have. As it was, she thought of sixteen things she wanted to say, but decided all of them would have to wait. "It's obvious you're spoiling for a fight, Matt. But you're just going to have to wait until we get to my house, because I refuse to fight in a car going sixty-five miles an hour on a crowded freeway!" And so saying, she turned and stared out her window.

With an angry flick of his wrist, he switched on the radio, and loud jazz music blasted through the car.

Paula winced. But she would no more have thought of asking him to lower the volume than she would have jumped out of the car and into the middle of traffic.

For the rest of the drive to her townhouse, they didn't speak to each other. The car reverberated with the pounding beat of the jazz band, and with each mile that ticked away, Paula's heart beat harder. She was so angry she felt like spitting, and she fully intended to give Matt Norman a piece of her mind at the first opportunity!

Finally they reached her street. He pulled up in front of the townhouse and switched off the ignition. Blessed quiet rained down on them. For a long moment, neither one moved. Then Paula yanked open her door and scrambled out of the car. She heard Matt not far behind her.

"Where do you think you're going?" he asked as he grabbed her arm, jerking her around to face him.

She nearly lost her balance and had to steady herself by placing her hands on his chest. She could feel his heart hammering against her palms. She raised her face. The full moon shone brightly in the clear, starry night. Somewhere in the distance a siren wailed. Paula caught a whiff of Matt's cologne: a crisp, woodsy scent. She trembled, her emotions in turmoil.

"I'd like to—" he said through clenched teeth.

"You'd like to what?" she demanded.

"I'd like to shake you until your teeth rattle," he said menacingly. Then, before she knew what was happening, his arms were around her, and his head had lowered, his mouth capturing hers. Her heart thundered in her ears as his hands slipped under her jacket and found her bare back. A shudder raced through her as her body molded against his, and she felt the heat and hardness of his length against her.

She clung to him, head whirling as his tongue delved and explored her mouth and his hands stroked her back, then slipped lower. She could feel the moan deep within her at the heated caress, and her arms tightened around his neck, one hand sliding into his thick hair.

"You're driving me crazy," he muttered against her mouth. She knew, from the ragged sound of his breathing and thickness of his voice, that it took almost a superhuman effort for him to drag his mouth away from hers, to loosen his hold on her.

"We have to talk," he said. "But not out here."

Silently, they walked to the door. Paula stumbled once, and Matt steadied her. A bewildering array of emotions churned inside her: anger, confusion, excitement, fear—and a quivering need deep in her belly.

Once inside, Paula took off her jacket and laid it neatly over the cherrywood table as she stalled for time to get herself under control once more. She'd left a lamp on in the foyer, but Matt stood out of the reach of its dim glow, his face in the shadows.

"I apologize for my behavior out there." He motioned toward the door.

"What about your behavior at the party?" she countered.

"*My* behavior at the party?" He ran his hands through his hair.

Paula already knew him well enough to know that when he ran his hands through his hair, he was frustrated or exasperated, or both.

"You're a good one to talk," he continued. "Your behavior was embarrassing."

"Embarrassing!" She glared at him.

"Throwing yourself at Rory all night, hanging on

every word; you were *my* date, and you embarrassed me."

"You, you—" Paula sputtered, so angry she could hardly speak. "You—bastard!"

"If my mother could see you now, she wouldn't be so charmed, would she?" His lip curled as they glared at each other.

"*You're* the one who ignored *me* all night. *You're* the one who walked away and left me with your *friend*. *You're* the one who embarrassed *me*, not the other way around!" Paula shouted, advancing on Matt with each word she spoke until she was standing close enough to jab him in the chest with her finger.

Suddenly a whirlwind flew between them, and Paula jumped back.

"Ow! Goddammit! That monster bit me!" Matt hopped around on one leg while holding the other.

Paula's eyes widened as she saw Miss Milly hissing at Matt, teeth bared. Paula bent down and scooped up the cat. "She was just trying to protect me," she explained. "Did she hurt you?"

"Damn right she hurt me! She should be locked up! She's a danger to society!" He sank onto the ladder-back chair sitting next to the cherrywood table and examined his left ankle. "There are teeth marks on my ankle!"

"There's no need to keep carrying on like that," Paula said calmly. Men could be such babies sometimes, she thought. "I'll go put Miss Milly into my bedroom and shut the door. Then I'll bring you a Band-Aid."

When she returned to the foyer, Matt was still rubbing his ankle and muttering to himself. He looked up, his green eyes flashing daggers at her.

Paula calmly handed him the bandage. "If you hadn't yelled at me, this never would have happened."

He glared at her, then said through clenched teeth, "I should have known you'd try to make this look like it was my fault."

"Well, it *was* your fault," Paula said, wondering why it was that men were so unreasonable.

Matt rolled his eyes heavenward. "I give up. I can't win, so why do I even try?" He put the bandage on his ankle, then lowered his cuff. He stood. "Look," he said, making a visible effort to speak quietly, "why don't we just admit we've made a mistake, cut our losses, and say good-bye with some dignity?"

Good-bye? Did that mean what she thought it meant? "Fine," she snapped. "That's fine with me."

"Good." He brushed at his pants, straightened his jacket, and avoided her eyes. "Well—"

"Thank you for a lovely evening, Mr. Norman," she said, sarcasm dripping from her tongue. "I had *such* a wonderful time. You're *such* a wonderful host—so solicitous, so attentive, so gentlemanly." *Stuffed shirt. Horse's ass. Arrogant, stupid, fool.* She gave him her sweetest smile. *I hope you get gangrene from Miss Milly's bite. I hope your leg falls off.* "Now, drive carefully, y'hear?" she drawled in her best southern-belle voice.

She marched to the door, yanked it open, stuck her chin up in the air, and waited for him to walk out.

Then she slammed the door as hard as she could.

Matt muttered all the way home. Damned infuriating woman! What was wrong with her? Why couldn't she act like a normal, reasonable human being? Well, it just reinforced his opinion that most women were overly emotional anyway and didn't understand the concept of logic or reason. They led with their feelings, said anything that popped into their heads, were always trying to catch you off balance, and they didn't play fair. And they *loved*, absolutely *loved* to use sex against you. Anytime they could, they wore clothes that were designed especially to turn on every male within two hundred miles—just as Paula had tonight—and they wore perfume that was calculated to scramble your brains, and they never missed a chance to flirt with you and tease you and drive you nuts.

And Paula Romano was the worst of the worst. The way she'd fallen all over Rory tonight only proved it. God, he'd had a narrow escape. To think that last night—and even tonight when he'd thought first Lucia Garibaldi, then Simon Whittaker, were picking on her—he'd begun to soften toward her, to think maybe, just maybe, the two of them might have something going for them. It certainly was a good thing she'd shown her true colors before he'd made a complete ass of himself.

Women like Paula Romano were all the same. They enjoyed keeping a man in turmoil. They actually *liked* to fight.

Matt hated to fight.

His mind turned longingly toward Sarah Whittaker. Toward her softness, her gentleness, her calmness. True, she didn't turn him on, but maybe he could learn to feel that way about her. Then he grimaced. He knew darn well he would never feel anything other than friendship for Sarah.

He also knew something else. Sarah might be wrong for him, but Paula was equally wrong for him. The best thing he could do for himself would be to put her out of his mind and out of his life. Completely.

*   *   *

"Hey, buddy, how's it going?" Rory asked as he and Matt passed each other in the hallway Monday morning on the way to their respective offices. "How was your weekend?"

"Fine."

"I really had a good time Saturday night," Rory said.

Was he born in a good mood? "Great. Glad to hear it."

"I *really* liked Paula."

"That was obvious."

"Well, you *said* you're not interested in her, didn't you?" Rory grinned, a smirk on his face that Matt didn't like one bit.

"That's exactly right. I'm *not* interested in her. The field is entirely free."

Rory pursed his lips. "You sure?"

"Absolutely sure."

"So you really don't mind if I call her up and ask her for a date?" Another smirk.

"Why should I mind?" One of these days somebody was going to punch out Rory's lights. Hell, why *should* he mind? It might do Rory some good to come up against a hellcat like Paula. After a few dates with her, he might not look so smug and self-satisfied. Then Matt grinned. Maybe that other hellcat, the one she called Miss Milly, would give Rory rabies.

"Well, I'm glad to see you're smiling. I guess that means you probably won't mind giving me her phone number either, right?"

The smile faded. Matt stared at Rory. If they hadn't been friends for so long, he'd think Rory was deliberately pushing him. "Be glad to. Come into my office. I'll give it to you right now."

*   *   *

By Monday afternoon Paula finally calmed down. And unfortunately, for some stupid reason, she was beginning to think maybe she'd been just a teensy weensy bit in the wrong. The question was, did she care enough about Matt to do anything about it? Because she knew someone like Matt Norman would not swallow his pride and make the first move toward her, even if he were regretting his actions of Saturday night.

She thought about him and their situation for the rest of the day. By the time she got home that night, she still hadn't decided what she wanted to do.

At seven o'clock, she was just sitting down to her dinner of a broiled chicken breast and a salad when the phone rang. *Maybe it's Matt,* she thought, as she raced for the phone.

But it wasn't. It was Rory Sebastian.

He asked her out to dinner the following Saturday night. When she didn't answer immediately, he said, "What's the matter? You act surprised."

"I am surprised. I thought you and Matt were such good friends."

"We *are* good friends."

"In my crowd, a good friend wouldn't do this behind his friend's back."

"Matt gave me his permission."

Paula felt like the breath had been knocked out of her. "Matt gave you his permission," she echoed.

A low chuckle. "That's what I said."

"You *asked* him if you could call me?"

"Yup."

"And he gave you his permission." Paula knew she sounded dumbstruck, but that's the way she felt. Of course, she'd known Matt was angry with her. But to give Rory his *permission* to call her, as if she were some kind of chattel!

Another low chuckle. "He said he didn't care."

Paula took a deep breath. She spoke carefully, slowly. "Well, Rory, this may come as a surprise to you and to Matt, but I make my own decisions, and I'm not interested in going out with you."

"And here I thought we got along so well the other night."

He didn't sound the least upset. In fact, he sounded as if he were teasing her. If Paula hadn't known the behavior was childlike, she would have stamped her foot. First Matt said he didn't care about her; now Rory wasn't even disappointed that she'd turned him down. She was definitely losing her touch.

"Well, you can't blame a guy for trying," he said.

No, but you could blame the guy's friend for encouraging him, Paula thought.

"Listen, Rory, thanks for the invitation," she finally said, "but I'm really busy right now. I've got to go."

"Paula?"

"Yes?"

"Before we hang up, there's one more thing I'd like to say."

Paula sighed. Now what?

The laughter in his voice had completely disappeared. "Matt cares," Rory said softly. "But he's doing his best to pretend he doesn't."

Then he hung up, and Paula stood there staring at the phone.

SIX

On Wednesday morning about eleven Rachel brought a Federal Express package into Matt's office. He reached for it absently, then handed her a sheaf of papers.

"Would you make those corrections, please?" He didn't look up from the deposition he was reading.

"Certainly."

It was nearly noon when Matt finally remembered the package. He pulled the strip across the top, removing the white envelope inside. Reaching for his letter opener, he slit the top of the envelope. When he saw the pale-blue stationery with the darker blue scalloped edge, his hand stilled, and he stared at the paper. What was she up to now?

Like a marionette whose actions are guided by someone else, he slowly opened the folded note. There was one sentence on the page.

Rory's not the one I want.

It was very quiet in the office. The grandfather clock that graced the corner of his office—the one Matt had not been able to resist, even though he'd paid far too much for it—chimed the hour. He could hear his heart beating. He stared at the sentence so long the words blurred.

Still moving in slow motion, he picked up the discarded Fed Ex container and threw it in his wastebasket. Then he slowly refolded the note and held it over the wastebasket. A shaft of sunlight danced over his hand as it hovered there. He released the note, and it fluttered down, settling softly on top of the other trash. Matt stared at it for a second, then resolutely looked away.

An hour later, he was still acutely aware of the blue paper beckoning to him from the wastebasket. He lowered the mike from his dictating equipment. Cursing the day that damned dog had run in front of Paula's truck, he bent down, scooped up the note, and tucked it into his breast pocket.

"You sent Matt Norman a note saying Rory Sebastian isn't the one you want?" Kim's voice rose to a near-squeak as she stared at Paula. The two of them were sitting in a booth at Chili's after stuffing themselves on curly fries and hamburgers.

"Yes." Paula nodded to the young waiter who had a big pitcher of iced tea. He refilled her glass, then refilled Kim's.

"So what do you think he'll do?" Kim asked as she stirred a packet of sweetener into her glass.

"I honestly don't know." Paula rubbed her stomach. "God, I'm full. Why did you let me eat so much?"

"As if I could have stopped you!" Kim made a face. "There's no one on God's green earth—including me—who can stop you from doing anything you want to do, and you know it. You're the most determined, stubborn person I know."

"Thanks." Paula laughed at the look on Kim's face.

"That wasn't meant to be a compliment," Kim said dryly.

"I didn't think it was. But I liked it anyway."

Kim grinned. "Quit changing the subject. I'll amend my question. What are you *hoping* he'll do?"

Paula shrugged. "I'm hoping he'll come to his senses and see that he's as attracted to me as I am to him. I'm hoping he'll recognize his reaction on Saturday night for just what it was—jealousy. I'm hoping he'll swallow his pride now that I've made the first move and call me."

"And if he doesn't?"

"I'm betting he will."

"But just supposing he doesn't see the light. Are you going to forget about this whole wacky scheme?"

Paula shrugged again. "I haven't thought that far ahead."

"Come on, Paula, I know you too well, remember?"

Paula smiled. "Okay. If he doesn't—well, then, I guess I'll just have to think of something else to do."

Kim's blue eyes sparkled as she leaned forward. "I knew it. That poor guy doesn't stand a chance."

Matt still hadn't called by Friday afternoon. She decided she'd give him until Sunday. If he still hadn't called her by then, she'd have to decide on an alternate action.

She smiled as she pulled into the driveway of Mr. T.'s house. She hoped he was home this week.

He was. He walked out onto the driveway and unlocked the gates barring entrance to the back of the property so that she could pull the truck closer to the pool area.

"Hello, Paula." Shading his eyes with his hand, he

watched her climb out of the truck. He was dressed in his usual Friday-afternoon outfit: worn jeans, beat-up cowboy boots, and faded plaid flannel shirt. On his compact, muscular frame, the outfit looked completely natural, as if he'd been born working the open range—and indeed, he had.

"Hi, Mr. T." She stuck out her hand, and he clasped it warmly. He wasn't very tall, so her eyes were almost on a level with his as they smiled at each other. "I missed you last week."

"Couldn't be helped." A shadow passed over his face, momentarily dimming his smile.

Paula studied him thoughtfully as he helped her unload her supplies. He looked preoccupied, troubled even. She hoped nothing was seriously wrong. As she worked, he stood nearby, and for a while they talked about his winter garden. He proudly pointed out the potatoes, onions, and tomatoes that would be harvested in early spring about the time most people began to think of planting.

Then he fell silent. Paula glanced up at him several times while she worked, and each time he was staring off into space, his mouth set in a grim line. Finally, she asked, "Something bothering you, Mr. T.?"

He pursed his lips. After a moment, he said, "Yes. And I'd like to talk to you about it. You're young. Maybe you can be more objective about this than I can." He gestured toward the patio furniture on his back veranda. "Let's go sit over there for a minute."

Paula covertly glanced at her watch. She had some time. Once they were seated he leaned forward, propping his elbows on his knees. He didn't look at her as he talked.

"I'm having a problem with my David."

David? Paula could hardly believe it. David, who

was Mr. T.'s only child, was a paragon, according to his father who had proudly boasted of David's many accomplishments.

"He's involved with an unsuitable woman, and I don't know what to do about it."

Paula made an encouraging murmur, not sure what else to say.

"She's got him so besotted, he doesn't know which end is up. He's talkin' about marrying her, and I won't have it!"

Paula cringed at his tone, wondering if he'd talked that way to David. She hoped not. David was thirty years old and certainly capable of making his own decisions. "What's wrong with this woman?" she asked softly.

"Everything!"

"Could you be more specific?"

He sighed. "Well, for one thing, she's been married before and she has a child."

"Well . . ." How to begin, she wondered. "You know, Mr. T., lots of people have been married and no longer are. Sometimes it's not their fault that things went wrong. You're such a fair man, it's hard to believe you'd hold that against her."

"That's not all," he snapped.

"Why don't you tell me everything, then?"

"She's a singer, for God's sake! She sings in some *club* in Montrose."

Paula almost smiled. His inflection suggested that this poor woman spent her time working in the deepest recesses of hell.

"There's nothing wrong with being a singer," she said. She hesitated for a minute. "I've sung in a lot of clubs around town myself."

His head whipped around, startled gray eyes staring at her. His face was a mask of disbelief.

"It's true," she said softly. "My real love is music. I only do this . . ." She gestured toward the pool. "—To pay the rent and buy groceries, but my goal is to become a paid composer."

"I thought—"

"I know what you thought. But, as you can see, things are not always what they seem." She leaned forward, earnestness tinging her voice. "A woman who has a child to raise might not have as many options open to her as a woman with no obligations. Besides, there's nothing wrong with being a singer. Why don't you give the poor girl a chance? Why jump to the conclusion that she's not suitable without even meeting her, talking to her?"

"I have no desire to meet her," he said stiffly, now refusing to meet Paula's eyes.

"Mr. T.," she said softly, "I thought you were a fair man."

"I *am* a fair man!" He jumped up and paced toward the pool.

Paula followed him, but more slowly, giving him time to cool down. She knew one of his greatest attributes was also his greatest fault—his tenacity. Although this trait had stood him in good stead when it came to building a fortune and carving a place for himself in the upper echelons of Houston's business community, it also kept him from being as open-minded as he could have been, because once he took a stand, he tended to stick with it regardless of what others might say. He was also very proud, and admitting he might be mistaken would be difficult for him.

"Has David ever given you cause for concern before?" she asked.

"No." His answer was muffled, and he didn't turn around.

"Isn't he level-headed, with lots of common sense?" She was quoting Mr. T.'s exact words.

He nodded, finally turning to look at her.

"Why are you so certain he's making a mistake then?"

He shrugged. "It's just that I had such high hopes for David."

"I know."

"I wanted him to marry someone special—someone who came from a certain background."

Paula patted his shoulder. "Someone just like your own wife . . ." She let her voice trail off.

His gray eyes were inscrutable. "My wife was *very* special." His voice was deceptively soft.

Paula knew he was angry. "I never said she wasn't."

"You know damn well what kind of background both she and I came from."

Of course she'd known. He'd bragged about being self-made, about how he and his beloved Emily had worked side by side to build what they had, how they'd both come from nothing.

"Emily would have fit in anywhere. She was a lady, the kind that's born, and it wouldn't have mattered where she came from—she would still have been a lady."

"I rest my case," Paula said.

Late that afternoon, as Matt prepared to leave the office, his mother walked in unannounced.

"Rachel said no one was with you, so I thought I'd come in and see you for a minute," she announced breezily.

As usual, she looked great, Matt thought. Today she

was dressed in a beautifully cut pumpkin-colored suit of some sort of soft wool. The jacket was open revealing a black silk blouse adorned simply with a strand of creamy pearls. He'd never known his mother to wear the wrong thing.

She settled herself gracefully in one of the chairs in front of his desk, crossed her legs, and smiled. "I haven't talked to you all week."

Matt tensed. "I've been very busy, Mother."

"Darling," she said, "I wasn't rebuking you. I was simply stating a fact."

Matt could feel his stomach knotting. Why did she do this to him? His father could have stated the same fact, and it wouldn't have bothered Matt at all. But his mother was a different story. She'd always had this effect on him. She always made him feel defensive, and then he did or said something childish, and *then* he felt guilty because he knew he'd overreacted to her. But not this time, he vowed. He would not let her provoke him today.

"I thought last weekend's party turned out very well, didn't you?" she asked brightly.

"Yes, it was nice," he lied.

"I enjoyed seeing your Paula again."

"Mother . . ." He struggled to keep from showing her how frustrated he felt. "She isn't *my* Paula."

"Oh, you know what I meant, dear."

Oh, he knew what she meant, all right.

"I like that girl," she continued. "Although at one time, your father and I hoped you and Sarah might get together, I've come to realize Sarah is completely wrong for you."

Matt knew he should keep his mouth shut. If he just nodded agreeably, his mother would eventually leave.

But even as he told himself to ignore her, he blurted, "And you think Paula is *right* for me?"

"Matt, you're putting words in my mouth. All I said was that I like the girl."

"Why don't *you* date her then?" *Oh, great. That was a mature thing to say!* He could feel himself flushing.

"Now, Matt . . ." Amusement flickered deep in her eyes.

"You made your point." Why didn't she just leave?

She sighed and stood up, smoothing down her skirt. She looked at him for a long moment, then walked around the desk, leaned down and hugged him. "I'm sorry, Matt," she said. "This is none of my business. You're perfectly right to be annoyed with me. I don't blame you at all."

As she walked out of his office, Matt slumped back in his chair. She'd done it again. He felt as guilty as hell.

SEVEN

By eleven o'clock Sunday morning Paula was certain Matt wasn't going to call. She'd been so sure sending him that Federal Express package would do the trick, but five days had gone by since she'd sent the note, and she still hadn't heard from him.

Wasn't that just like a man? she thought in disgust. Letting pride stand in the way of them doing something they really wanted to do? Women were so much more reasonable when it came to admitting they were wrong. Men were all alike. Mr. T.—making himself miserable over his son, and Matt—making both her *and* himself miserable!

Well, if he wasn't going to call her on his own, she'd just have to nudge him a bit. But how? That might require some thought. She always did her best thinking when she was exercising. Shedding the clothes she'd worn to church, she put on a leotard and tights, then inserted a Jane Fonda workout tape into her VCR. Soon she was bouncing along with Jane, working up a good sweat and plotting her strategy.

Twenty minutes into the workout, her phone rang.

She stopped, heart and pulse racing from the exercise, sweat slick against her skin. She turned down the sound on the TV, then walked to the phone while she tried to catch her breath.

On the fourth ring, she picked it up. "Hello?"

"Paula?"

It was Matt.

A current of excitement shimmered through her. "Hi, Matt," she said, still breathing hard.

"You sound as if you've been running."

"Not running—exercising."

"That's good. Everyone should exercise."

"Yes, I think so, too." *Good grief, listen to them!*

"So how have you been?"

She had to stifle her laughter. It was obvious to her that he was trying to sound offhand and casual, just as she was. Two adults with no more composure than teenagers. "I've been fine. How about you?"

"Oh, I've been fine, too. Busy, of course."

"Oh, of course. Me, too." She tapped her foot. This was ridiculous. She knew he hadn't called to make small talk. Should she break the ice first?

"The weather's been great, hasn't it?'

"Wonderful." *As if I care about the weather.*

"Paula—"

"Matt—"

They spoke at the same time. Then they both laughed.

"You go ahead," he said.

"No, *you* go ahead," she said.

"I got your note." His voice sounded husky.

Her stomach felt hollow. "I figured you did." Now her voice sounded odd. *Why are you nervous?* Suddenly this no longer seemed like a game. Suddenly it was as if she really cared what Matt Norman thought of her.

He cleared his throat. "Would you like to do something with me today?"

Warmth filled the hollow space. She felt a smile spread across her face. "What did you have in mind?"

"I don't care. Whatever you want to do is fine with me."

"You really don't care where we go?"

"No."

"Well, in that case, my father offered me two tickets to the Oilers game. It starts at three. How does that sound?"

"Uh . . . an Oilers game?"

He didn't sound very excited. Paula thought he'd be thrilled to go. She'd never met a man who didn't love football. "Yes. They're good seats, too." She hoped her father hadn't given the tickets to someone else.

"Well, if that's what you want to do."

He still sounded less than enthusiastic. "I thought you'd be excited about going," she said. "Oh. You probably go all the time. It's old hat to you, is that it?"

"Actually, I've never been to an Oilers game."

Paula was astounded. Never been to an Oilers game! Where had he been living the past ten years? On Mars? "Then it's high time you did go. Are you one of those people who'd much rather watch them play on television?"

"Not really." He laughed. "Listen, it's not important. If you want to go, then that's what we'll do. What time will we have to leave?"

"No later than two o'clock."

"Okay. I'll see you at two."

Matt didn't expect to enjoy himself at the game—not only because he hated football but because he'd hoped to have some quiet time with Paula. He wanted to talk, and the circuslike atmosphere of a professional football game wasn't what he had in mind.

Matt preferred less noisy spectator sports like tennis and golf, although when it came down to it, he would rather be a participant than a spectator of *any* sport. He didn't mind an occasional baseball game, which he considered a clean, intelligent sport, but football? It was his personal opinion that there was nothing entertaining or interesting about a bunch of grown men trying to kill each other. He knew he was in the minority in Houston. Texans considered football right up there next to religion. So he usually kept his opinions to himself.

But today he was getting a big kick out of watching Paula. He'd made up his mind before he called her that no matter what happened today, no matter where they went or what they did, he was just going to relax and enjoy himself. And he was doing just that. And it was fun. Especially watching Paula.

Right now her face was flushed and excited, her cheeks bright, her eyes sparkling. The crowd and noise and color suited her. She'd been jumping up and down, waving her blue-and-white pom pom and laughing and yelling. Even when the crowd sang that corny fight song, she didn't seem the least bit embarrassed by its terrible lyrics and sang right along.

"I love this!" she yelled in his ear. "Don't you?" She had just finished a big container of nachos, and she licked cheese off her fingers with gusto.

He didn't know where she put all the food. The nachos were the last in a long line of junk food she'd consumed throughout the first half. It certainly didn't show anywhere. In fact, she looked great. She wore snug jeans and a blue Oilers T-shirt that molded to her slim curves. On her head sat a jaunty blue cowboy hat, and her wild hair curled around her animated face. He had a sudden mental picture of Sarah Whittaker, whom he'd never seen in a pair of jeans.

"That's quite a hat," he remarked.

"My Oilers hat," Paula bragged. "It's a good-luck charm. When I wear it, they win. When I don't, they lose."

"Is that why they lost last week?"

"Wouldn't surprise me." Then she gave him a sly look. "I thought you didn't pay any attention to the Oilers!"

He grinned. "I may not be crazy about football, but I don't live in a vacuum."

"It's hard for me to believe you don't like football."

"You've said that at least ten times today," he said, frowning at her, but he wasn't really annoyed. It was quite pleasant to tease her. She had an enchanting smile, with those irresistible dimples, and when he teased her, she always smiled up at him.

Her smile did curious things to him. It made him want to scoop her up in his arms and kiss her. Funny, he thought. From the moment he'd met her, in spite of wanting to throttle her, he'd wanted to kiss her.

But even as she attracted him with her smile and her sexy body and amused him with her oddball ideas, he couldn't imagine living with someone like her. She would wear him out.

Of course, he had to admit he'd thought about her constantly this past week. She was like the green grass on the other side of the fence. Different, so more appealing. She was like caffeine. Something he knew wasn't good for him, but he craved it anyway. She was like chocolate—a taste only whet his appetite for more.

Like chocolate . . . Perhaps he would simply have

to gorge himself—spend so much time with her that they would finally become sick of each other. There was no doubt in his mind that this would happen eventually. Once the excitement of the unknown had worn off, what would be left?

Paula wouldn't be able to stand his staid existence over a long period of time any more than he'd be able to cope with her unbridled enthusiasms, which seemed to be at opposite ends of the pole to his—a point that had been emphasized earlier when she'd talked about her family.

"I owe you a debt of thanks," she'd said as they were driving to the Dome.

"Oh?" He slanted a look at her.

"Yes, because we had this date, I didn't have to do the usual Sunday afternoon dinner at my folks."

He nodded, although he rarely had Sunday-afternoon dinner with his own parents. Instead, about twice a month, the three of them had dinner together during the week. He supposed it was the same thing, though.

"All my brothers come, along with their wives, and usually there are several aunts and uncles and cousins. It's not unusual for my mother to feed twenty people," Paula said. "It's like a zoo."

"Sounds like a lot of work." It gave him a headache to imagine twenty people for dinner every single Sunday.

"I'm sure it is, but you don't know my mother. She thrives on that kind of stuff. You wouldn't believe the amount of food we consume." She ticked the items off on her fingers. "Antipasto, followed by pasta with meatballs and sausage and Italian bread, then a meat course with potatoes and vegetables, then dessert."

"Jesus," Matt said softly. "Are you serious?"

"Would this face lie to you?" She mugged for him.

"And after that we all watch football and yell at the referees, not to mention the players and coach."

Even though she was pretending she didn't like the Sunday routine, Matt could tell she really did. If he and Paula were to become serious about each other—which of course would never happen—he tried to imagine himself part of the scene she had just described. Having Sunday dinner at her parents' house week after week, watching football with her brothers and father, eating enormous meals. He shuddered. He was sure they were all very nice people, but even the idea exhausted him. He thought of his quiet house with its high ceilings and banks of windows overlooking the bayou and flower-filled courtyard.

His favorite kind of Sunday consisted of getting up early, reading the Sunday paper while having two cups of coffee and maybe some raisin toast or a bagel. Then midmorning he usually met Rory for a couple games of tennis at the club. Then if they felt like it they'd go to lunch together.

The rest of the day he liked to putter around the house: listen to music, read, catch up on paperwork. Sunday nights he almost always went to bed early. He liked starting his week off feeling fresh and rested. When you were in line for a senior partnership, you didn't stay out half the night, then go to work the next day and expect to perform at your peak.

He looked at Paula, who was on her feet shouting at the referee. He had a feeling Paula didn't know the meaning of a calm, ordered existence. Just look at her. She couldn't keep still. She was on her feet more than she was in her seat.

"Did I tell you about singing the National Anthem at one of these games last year?" she shouted over the din of the crowd.

"Yes."

She grinned, obviously pleased with herself. Then she jumped up. "Block, you lunkhead!" She turned toward Matt. "Honestly, I think I could play better than some of these guys. I should've been born a boy!"

Matt smiled indulgently. She was like an endearing child in her exuberance. Maybe, like a child, she just needed teaching. Perhaps once she was introduced to a more orderly existence, she would enjoy it. Since he'd already decided the only way to handle his attraction to her was to indulge it until it ran its course, why not try to educate her? Maybe even change her. He thought it would be quite pleasant to introduce her to his world and the things he liked to do.

Yes, he liked that plan. It made perfect sense. It was always better to think things out like this. That way you didn't do anything you'd regret later.

As for today, he'd take her home and he'd apologize for his behavior after the dinner party. He'd tell her he really did enjoy her company and that he hoped they could continue to see each other. He'd tell her he wanted to be her friend, and he hoped she felt the same way.

But under no circumstances would he give her more than a friendly good-night kiss. Kissing her seemed to muddle his thinking. And now that he had the situation under control, he wanted to keep it that way.

Paula slid into the passenger seat of Matt's BMW, which he'd told her he'd gotten back earlier in the week, and slanted a look at him. He certainly was good to look at, even if she wished he'd loosen up a bit. He was so *conservative*. Take the clothes he wore. There wasn't anything really *wrong* with what he had on today, except that it was so boring. Gray wool slacks with a razor-sharp crease, darker gray crew-neck sweater, polished black loafers, and gray socks. Mr. Up-and-coming-lawyer himself. Yuppie all the way, right down to the shining BMW.

Paula tried to imagine Matt with dirt on his hands and sweat soaking through his clothes. She tried to picture him in tight jeans and tighter T-shirt, maybe wearing cowboy boots or a black leather bomber jacket. She couldn't.

She tried to imagine him sitting in a crowded club watching her sing, with the music ricocheting off the walls and smoke curling through the air, or the two of them zooming around on a big Harley-Davidson motorcycle. She couldn't.

She tried to imagine him spending other Sundays watching football games, eating spaghetti, laughing and carrying on with her family, or going with her to a Save the World rally or an outdoor rock festival in Austin. She couldn't.

So what on earth was she doing here?

She looked out the window. Why couldn't she just forget about him? Was she just turned on by the challenge? Buoyed by the idea of a conquest like Matt Norman? Was she that shallow?

Lord, she hoped not. She peeked at him again, watched as his strong hands expertly maneuvered the car through the chaos that was the Dome parking lot after a game. That funny, hollow feeling was back in her stomach again.

If she were perfectly honest with herself, the reason she continued to pursue Matt Norman was because he turned her on. Not only turned her on, but turned her inside out. Stupid or not, cliché or not, she had wanted him from the first moment she'd laid eyes on him. She wondered if he had ever lived with anyone. She wondered what it would feel like to have him make love to her. She wondered if she was making a big mistake.

She didn't want to hurt him. And she certainly didn't want to get hurt. She just wanted . . . What? To be with him, to see if what she felt for him was more than just her hormones acting up because he was such a gorgeous, sexy man.

Why shouldn't they enjoy each other? she rationalized. They were two healthy, grown-up people. If they were attracted to each other and wanted to go to bed together, there was no reason they shouldn't. She was being silly, worrying about how different they were. Neither one of them was seriously considering the other on any sort of permanent basis. Matt knew the score as well as she did. There was no doubt in her mind that he was probably even now thinking the same thoughts she was.

Besides, he was too straight-laced. Spending time with her would be good for him. He needed educating, loosening up. And she was just the person to show him what he'd been missing. She'd teach him to learn how to have fun.

As if he could read her mind, he said, "Did you have fun today?" They had finally escaped the crush of cars on Kirby Drive, and the BMW gathered speed as Matt entered the ramp for the 610 Loop.

"I had a great time. How about you?"

"It was more fun than I thought it would be."

See? she thought.

"Tell me more about your family," he said as they cruised smoothly along 610. He switched on the radio, and soft music surrounded them.

It was already dark, and the interior of the car seemed snug and intimate to Paula. She lay her head back against the headrest, turning so she could watch

Matt drive. His profile looked clear and strong against the lights winking by them. No question about it. She didn't think she'd ever get tired of looking at him.

"What do you want to know?" she asked.

"How many brothers and sisters do you have?"

"I have four brothers."

"Four brothers!"

Paula grimaced. "Yeah, and believe me, many's the day I've wished I were an only child."

"That's funny. I've always wished I had a brother."

"If you'd spent your childhood getting your pigtails pulled and frogs put in your bed and people sneaking into your room and reading your diary, you'd change your tune," Paula said.

Matt chuckled. "Well, tell me about your brothers anyway."

So she did. She told him about Frankie, the oldest, and Joey, the next in line, and Rocky, the youngest. Then she told him about Tony. "Tony's always been a thorn in my side. He's very traditional and conservative. He'll make a wonderful accountant, I'm sure."

"You sound as if you think accounting is the most boring business in the world." He flicked on his turn signal and entered the ramp that connected the Loop with the Katy Freeway.

"I do," she said.

"But didn't you say you helped your father by keeping the books?"

"Right again."

Matt laughed. "You know, Paula," he said slowly, "you're the most inconsistent, unpredictable female I've ever known."

"Thank you." Paula was absurdly pleased, and she smiled at him.

He laughed again. "So if you're so turned off by accounting, why do you do it?"

"Somebody has to, and I have a head for figures," she said proudly. "I don't have to like it, do I?"

He shrugged. "I guess not."

Paula could tell by his tone of voice that he didn't know what to make of her reasoning. As far as she was concerned, it made perfect sense.

"But getting back to your brother," he continued, "surely you don't dislike him because he's studying accounting."

"I didn't say I disliked him . . . although . . ."

"Although, what?"

"Well, I love Tony. I really do. In fact, I love all my family. They're great. But Tony's like almost everyone else, except for my father. They all think they know best. My mother's always giving me these platitudes about life, always trying to make me into something I'm not. And Tony and Frankie and Joey and even Mary Ellen—she's Frankie's wife—they do the same thing. Try to force me into a mold I don't fit."

"Like what?"

"Well, my mother was upset when I quit teaching school. To her way of thinking, teaching is good training for marriage and having children."

"And you don't think so?"

"It's not that I don't. Teaching is fine if you like it. I didn't happen to like it. And as for getting married . . . well, I'd rather just have lovers."

Matt made a funny sound, as if he were choking.

"Are you okay?" she said. Had she shocked him?

"What about kids?" he finally said. "Are you against having kids, too?"

Here she was less sure of herself. "I do love kids,"

she admitted. "Well, I'll cross that bridge when I come to it."

"Hmm," he said.

This was going quite well, she thought. He was probably relieved to find out she wasn't going to try to worm a diamond and a proposal out of him. She had paved the way for them to become lovers quite nicely. Now he could do what she knew he wanted to do and not feel guilty about it.

"What do your father and brothers think of your ideas?" Matt asked after a long moment of silence.

"I . . . uh . . . really haven't told them exactly how I feel," Paula said sheepishly. "Well, actually, I haven't spelled it out for my mother, either." When he didn't say anything, she felt compelled to explain. "They simply wouldn't understand. It's easier to go along with them. My dad's understanding, but I'm not sure he'd understand this. And my brothers are *not* liberated. They're definitely the kind who think a woman's place is behind a hot stove."

"So their wives stay home."

"No. They work. But only because it's almost impossible nowadays to manage if you don't have two incomes coming in—not because Tony and Frankie like their wives working."

"What about the other brother—the one you said was married to the Scottish girl?"

"Joey? He's better. Elaine—his wife—is a computer genius, a whiz at math and science, and Joey's pretty proud of her." Paula smiled, thinking of her smart sister-in-law. "Actually, Elaine makes more money than Joey, which he's had a real hard time dealing with."

"That would be hard for any man to swallow."

"Why is it that no one seems to feel sorry for a

woman whose husband makes scads of money, but everyone feels sorry for a man whose wife is more successful than he is?" Only one more reason never to get married, Paula thought, because she had every intention of being wildly successful as well as rich.

"It's because that situation goes against the natural order of things," Matt said.

Paula's mouth dropped open. "I don't believe you said that. You mean you actually believe that women should be subservient to men? Even when it comes to the amount of money they make?"

"No. I only meant that for thousands of years, that's the way things have been. You women can't expect ingrained attitudes to change overnight. Besides, the nature of man is to go out and hunt for food. The nature of woman is to tend the cave, bear the children, and cook the food her man brings home."

"I don't *believe* this! Matt, this is the 1990's, not the *1*890's." She felt like laughing herself silly. Oh, he needed educating, all right.

"Some things never really change."

By now they'd reached her house. He glided the car to a smooth stop in front of the townhouse and turned off the ignition. Then he shifted in his seat so they were facing each other. She opened her mouth to say something else. There was nothing Paula liked better than a good, stimulating argument. Especially when she knew she'd win in the long run because she was right.

"Let's not argue," he said. "I hate arguments." He smiled—a slow, sexy smile—and Paula's heart flip-flopped, driving everything else out of her mind.

"You're not angry, are you?" His eyes glittered in the moonlight.

How could she stay angry with him? Even if he *did*

have the same chauvinistic attitude her brothers had. She should be used to it. She shook her head.

"Paula . . . I've been thinking . . ." He reached over and took her hand.

Paula's breath caught. Just a simple touch, but it had the power to render her speechless. His thumb rubbed against the back of her hand, and she trembled as chill-bumps broke out on her arms.

"Yes?"

"I—" He stopped, as if he'd lost his train of thought. "Let's go inside. For some reason, I can't think."

Once they were inside, she turned to face him. He stood with his back to the door; she stood a few inches away. Their eyes met.

"Paula . . ." His voice trailed off.

His eyes were flecked with gold. There was an expression in them that caused her heart to beat in heavy thuds. Even if she'd wanted to, she couldn't look away.

"Paula, I'm sorry about last week," he finally said.

"You should be," she said. But she was no longer angry with him. Actually, she just wanted him to kiss her.

He smoothed his hair back in that betraying nervous gesture he had. "I . . . uh . . . don't know why I acted that way."

"I think you do," she said, mesmerized by the shape of his mouth. In a minute, she was going to kiss him if he didn't shut up. "You were jealous."

He swallowed, and his Adam's apple bobbed. "I wasn't jealous."

He was so cute, she thought, when he was nervous. She liked it when he wasn't so sure of himself. It made him seem more approachable, sweet even. *Why didn't he kiss her?* He wanted to. She could see the desire in his eyes. She wet her lips and watched his gaze follow the path of her tongue. "I think you were, but that's okay. I kind of like the idea. It means you like me more than you're willing to admit."

"Of course I like you," he said, but he backed up. "In fact, I hope we can see a lot more of each other. I'd like us to be friends."

Friends? She wanted more than friendship. "Then why do you act as if you're afraid of me?" she challenged, feeling surer of herself now, knowing deep down that he not only liked her, he wanted her as much as she wanted him.

He stiffened. "I'm not afraid of you. I'm not afraid of anything."

"You're not?" She glided closer, placed her hands on his chest. She could feel his heart beating as fast as hers. "I'm glad," she murmured, raising her face.

"Well, uh, look, I think it's time I was going," he said. "I have a lot of work to get done before tomorrow morning." The words tumbled out like a rock slide down a mountain. "Good night, Paula. I'll call you tomorrow." He leaned down; his lips met hers lightly.

At the touch of his warm lips against hers, Paula closed her eyes and slid her arms around his neck. For one minute, he held back, then with a groan, his arms pulled her tight up against him, and he deepened the kiss.

Paula loved his kisses. She felt as if she were drowning in his kisses. She felt like she was in the middle of a whirlpool, spinning deeper and deeper into its vortex when he kissed her.

"Paula," he groaned as his mouth moved from her lips to her neck. His hands kneaded her back, then slipped under her T-shirt. She shuddered at the touch of his palms against her skin, and when they moved up her rib cage to touch her breasts, she gasped with pleasure.

"Matt," she whispered. Yes, this was what she wanted, what she'd *been* wanting.

He nuzzled her ear as his thumbs rubbed back and forth across the tightened nubs straining against her lacy bra. Paula's pulses raced, every nerve ending alive and tingling from the onslaught of sensations rushing through her body. She closed her eyes, all senses reeling under his intoxicating and insistent caresses. She could hear his ragged breathing, which matched her own. She moved against him in timeless invitation.

Then abruptly, shockingly, he stopped.

One minute he was making love to her, the next minute he was pulling her T-shirt down and holding her away from any contact with him, looking down at her with consternation written all over his face as he made a visible effort to bring himself under control. They were both breathing hard.

Paula stared at him. Heart racing, body trembling, her mind whirled in confusion. What was wrong with him?

Matt's face was flushed, his eyes twin magnets of fiery green as they burned into hers. A lock of his thick hair had tumbled across his forehead. He raised one hand to brush the offending hair back, and Paula's bewilderment was only intensified to see that his hand was shaking as much as her own insides.

"What's the matter, Matt?" she finally said.

She saw the muscles working in his throat as he swallowed. Any fool could see he was as affected by their aborted lovemaking as she was.

He took a deep breath. "I'm sorry, Paula. I lost control of myself, and I apologize."

"Apologize? There's nothing to apologize for. I wanted you to kiss me." She didn't know whether to be angry or amused.

"Yes, I know, and I . . . I wanted to kiss you, too, but I think we should go slowly. I think it's a mistake to let emotions take over like that. Before a man and woman—" He stopped, frowning. "Before a man and woman make love, they should talk about it and decide whether it's something they really want to do. They should have an understanding about it and what it means."

"Matt," Paula said patiently. "I don't think making love should go according to some set plan. Making love is all about feelings, and feelings can't be planned and ordered about. We both want to, and you know it."

"Just because a person wants something doesn't mean he should have it. People should be responsible for their actions."

"Are you worried that I'll expect something from you if we make love?"

His eyes narrowed. "No, Paula. That's not what's stopping me. You made yourself perfectly clear in the car. It's just that I don't believe in jumping into things. I'm a careful person. I like to know where I'm going before I begin."

"If you're too careful you might miss out on all the best things in life," she said. "I find it's much better to rely on my instincts and emotions."

"I'm sorry, but I don't operate that way," he insisted, his jaw set.

"Is that the lawyer or the man talking?" Paula was beginning to wonder if they would ever understand each other.

"It's both." His face and voice were so determined. "I'm sorry, but that's the way I feel. My credo has always been to think it through carefully before speaking or acting. And when I kiss you, I tend to—''

"Forget everything else?" she finished for him.

"Exactly."

He was so *earnest*. She smiled and touched his cheek. "There's nothing wrong with that, you know. Why can't we just enjoy each other and the way we're feeling right now? Why do we have to spoil it by analyzing it to death?"

For one brief moment, uncertainty flickered in his eyes as she caressed his cheek. Paula held her breath. Then Miss Milly meowed loudly, brushing against the backs of Paula's legs. Irritated by the interruption, Paula tried to shoo the cat away, but Miss Milly wouldn't go. In fact, she hissed at Matt, and the moment was gone.

"I'll call you tomorrow," he said.

Knowing she was beaten, at least for now, Paula bent down and picked up the cat, cradling her and whispering in her ear. "All right. And, Matt . . . ?"

He had already turned the doorknob, but he stopped.

"I had a wonderful time today. Thanks."

He turned, giving her a crooked smile—the one that made her insides turn to mush. Then he opened the door and was gone.

Paula stood with Miss Milly in her arms, burying her face in the cat's soft fur. "It's only the end of Round Two, Miss Milly," she murmured. "We've still got a heck of a long way to go!"

EIGHT

For the next two weeks, Paula sent Matt one red rose every single day. There was never any accompanying note, but he knew they had come from her. The first one only caused a few raised eyebrows. The second and third generated some snickers and knowing looks. The fourth and all the succeeding ones caused the entire office to buzz with amused gossip.

After the first week, Matt's father came in one morning, raised his eyebrows, and said, "What's going on, Matt?"

Matt sighed. "I don't know, Dad."

"You must know something." He advanced farther into the room and sat down. "Who's sending you the flowers?"

Matt sighed again. Part of him wished he had Paula's neck in his hands so he could strangle her; the other part was perversely pleased and flattered. "I think Paula is sending them, but I can't prove it."

His father's eyes twinkled. "You mean they're coming anonymously?"

"Yes." He had to look away. The look in his

father's eyes was unnerving. "Every time I've tried to talk to her about it, she just gives me this innocent look."

His father laughed. "The entire office is talking about it, you know."

"I know." Matt cringed, imagining what they were saying. "I'm sorry, Dad. I don't know what to do about it."

"Oh, hell, son, don't worry about it. I think it's funny." He stood up, still laughing.

Matt frowned. "But I thought you were upset, and that's why you came in."

"Shoot, no. I was just nosy, that's all."

Matt could hear him chuckling even after he'd closed the door behind him.

Rory was no less direct. "Hey, lover boy," he said as he poked his head into Matt's office. "Got your posy today?" Then he grinned. "Oh, yeah, there it is."

Matt now put his rose in a Waterford bud vase that sat on his desk where he could see it all day. What the hell, he figured. He might as well enjoy them. "Come on in," he said to Rory. "Close the door."

"So what's the deal?" Rory said as he slumped into a chair. "Are you being wooed by a fair lady?" He went into his Groucho Marx routine, waggling his eyebrows and all. "Anyone I know?"

"The roses are from Paula," Matt said.

Rory's eyes widened. A sly smile twisted his mouth. "Really? I thought it was all over between you two. I thought you couldn't stand her."

Matt shrugged.

"So are you two seeing each other now?"

"Yes, we're dating." They had been out three times in the past week, and Matt had had more fun than he'd ever had before—with anyone.

"So is it serious?" Rory's dark eyes glinted with curiosity.

"I don't know how I feel about her," Matt admitted truthfully. "I told myself I was only taking her out because I was curious about her. I figured I'd soon get sick of her."

Rory grinned. "But it hasn't happened."

Matt shook his head. "Not yet."

Rory's grin turned sly. "Did she tell you I called her?"

"More or less."

"You mad at me?"

"Have I acted as if I were?"

"No."

Matt decided he must be mellowing or something, because he wasn't even annoyed with Rory for sporting that knowing smile. "I encouraged you to call her," he said. "So how could I be mad?" There was no reason to tell Rory how jealous he'd felt.

"You're a bigger man than I am," Rory said. "If Paula were my girl, I'd keep her under wraps so no one else would even be tempted to call her."

And with that, he winked and left the office.

Paula was pleased with herself. She thought it had been a brilliant idea to send Matt the roses. She'd win this fight yet! The past two weeks had been wonderful, except that Matt was still determined to keep their relationship as casual as possible, and she was just as determined to get him into bed. But he had to think it was his decision.

She and Kim had been discussing the problem for the past hour.

"So where is Matt tonight?" Kim took a bite out of the Granny Smith apple she held.

Paula picked at a loose thread on the arm of Kim's paisley print sofa. A Roy Orbison song played softly on the tape deck. "He had some kind of a meeting."

"You know, Paula, I don't think you're going to be successful in this campaign of yours." Kim gave her apple a liberal dose of salt from a big porcelain salt shaker shaped like a fat pig. Then she took another bite. Juice dribbled down her chin, and she swiped it away with the back of her hand.

"Why do you say that?"

"Because I've worked at the firm for five years now, and everything I've ever seen or heard about Matt Norman tells me he won't change."

"He's already changing," Paula insisted. "He just doesn't know it."

"In what way?"

"Well, last night, for instance, we were supposed to go to some opening at one of the galleries, and I didn't feel like doing that. It was raining, and I didn't want to have to get dressed up, plus I was tired. Anyway, I called him, and he wasn't the least upset like I thought he'd be. You know how he always hates to have his schedule changed . . ."

Kim rolled her eyes. "Do I ever! And you should hear his secretary on the subject." She dropped the denuded apple core into an empty candy dish and set the salt shaker on her glass-topped coffee table. Crossing her legs Indian-fashion, she settled herself back in her chair.

For about the zillionth time, Paula wished she'd had the good fortune to be born with a face like Kim's. Even tonight, dressed in faded jeans and T-shirt, barefoot, devoid of makeup, she looked gorgeous. It would be easy to hate her, Paula thought, except no one hated Kim, not even women. Kim didn't have an insecure bone in her body, and she was the kind of person who always tried to make the people around her feel comfortable. And people responded to that generous quality.

"So what *did* you do last night?" she asked now.

Paula smiled, thinking of the night before. "We just stayed at my place," she said dreamily. "Built a fire, listened to Chopin—Matt loves Chopin—and we even roasted marshmallows." But at the end of the evening, he'd disappointed her again. What was his problem?

"Oh, spare me!" Kim said. "How corny can you get!"

"It wasn't corny. It was sweet."

"I have a hard time reconciling the Matt Norman I know and the word *sweet*." But Kim smiled.

"He *is* sweet."

"You know, Paula, I told you that goofy plan of yours would backfire on you, and it has."

Paula looked up. She frowned. "What do you mean?"

"Just what I said."

"But what do you *mean*?"

"I mean that it looks very much as if you've fallen for the guy—something I warned you against weeks ago."

"I have not!" Paula said indignantly. "I'm just having fun. But I have not fallen for him."

"Su-u-ure." Kim drawled the word knowingly.

"You don't have to say it that way, Kim. I mean it."

"Of course you mean it. That's why you have that sappy look on your face every time you say his name!"

"I do not!"

They stared at each other, and soon they were both laughing. Then, after they stopped and Paula caught her breath, she said, "Okay, so I like him a lot, and . . . I'm wildly attracted to him . . ."

"Yes?" Kim grinned.

"And I'm dying to have him make love to me," Paula finished in a rush. "However, that doesn't mean I'm in love or anything."

"Hey, I said I believed you, didn't I? Now, do you want to send out for a pizza?"

"With extra cheese and piles of mushrooms?" Paula said hopefully.

"Of course. Girls have to keep their strength up—" Kim started.

"—for the battle of the sexes!" Paula finished.

They fell into a fit of giggles. Then they called Domino's.

One Friday toward the end of November, Benjamin Tobias called Matt.

"Yes, Mr. Tobias?" Matt said once Rachel had put him on the line. "How are you?"

"I'm fine," Tobias said curtly. "The reason I called is because I've changed my mind about that new will."

"All right." Matt hoped he'd kept the surprise out of his voice.

"Yes, just leave the old will intact."

Matt made a notation on his daily reminder pad. "Okay, I'll take care of it."

"I suppose you're wondering why I changed my mind," Tobias said.

"Well, I'll admit I'm curious."

"I decided to give David's young woman a chance. Anyway, I've met her, and she seems to be all right."

"You've met her?"

"That's what I said, isn't it?"

"Just once?" Matt persisted doggedly, determined not to lose his temper.

"Once was enough," Tobias barked. "I didn't build up my business without learning a thing or two about human nature. I think I'm a good judge of character."

Matt sighed. "Well, it's your money."

"You still sound as if you think I'm doing the wrong thing," Tobias said, a hard edge to his voice.

Matt decided to plunge ahead, whether Tobias liked it or not. "Look, Ben, I thought you were wise to be skeptical and cautious. In fact, I would have gone a step further. I would have had the woman checked out. Even now it's not too late. I can arrange for a complete investigation of her, if you like. Then you can decide what you want to do based on facts." He wanted to add, "not hunches," but knew Tobias would blow his stack if he did.

"I trust my judgment, even if you don't."

Matt knew he'd annoyed the older man, but there was a lot of money and property involved; he had a duty to tell his client what he thought. "It's not a matter of judgment. As your lawyer, I have to recommend what I think is best, and I recommend a complete background check."

"I do *not* want a background check run on her!" Tobias snapped. Then he grumbled, "Smart young lawyers think they know everything!"

Damn, Matt thought. "Ben," he said soothingly, "that's what you're paying me for—my legal expertise. It's my obligation to advise you."

After they hung up, Matt sat and twirled his pen while he rehashed their conversation. Ever since he'd taken over Tobias's work, the older man had blown hot and cold. Matt knew Tobias had been suspicious of him at first, then for a while he'd seemed to trust him. Now their relationship was going backward, and once more Tobias was questioning Matt's counsel.

But Matt knew he was right about this. He'd felt Tobias's initial reaction to David's romantic involvement with this woman had been a kneejerk one, but this complete reversal based on no more than one meeting with the woman wasn't wise, either. Matt thought a complete investigation was justified as well as prudent. And knowing Tobias's history with the firm, he'd thought Tobias would agree. After all, his assets had taken years to build.

Matt swiveled his chair around so he could look out the window. The weather had turned pretty again, after weeks of intermittent rain. He stood up and walked to the window. He never tired of looking at Houston's skyline. He'd been to all the major cities in the United States, and he'd never seen one that could top it. Today the bright sun lit the sides of the glass buildings until it almost hurt his eyes to look at them.

He wished he could forget about Benjamin Tobias and the office and just pack up all his work and put it away until Monday morning. Looking at the aquamarine sky and knowing that the temperature was probably hovering around the sixties made him want to be outside breathing fresh air. He thought longingly of the golf course, of his clubs lying idle.

But he couldn't. He had work to do. There were still three important items left on his agenda for the day. And they couldn't be put off. Only undisciplined, self-indulgent people gave in to whims and ignored responsibility. And Matt wasn't one of them.

He sighed, turning back to his desk and the work facing him. As a matter of fact, he'd probably have to work late tonight because he and Paula were spending the day together tomorrow. Paula had wanted to drive to Galveston and spend the day walking the Strand and picnicking on the beach, but Matt had vetoed that idea.

"I haven't even begun my Christmas shopping yet," he'd explained, "and by this time I'm usually finished."

Paula had given him an astonished look. "But, Matt! It's only the middle of November!"

"When do *you* do your Christmas shopping?"

She shrugged, eyes dancing mischievously. "Usually the last two or three days before Christmas."

Oh, Lord, he thought. "Well, I don't believe in waiting until the last minute. I think a well-organized life makes for a well-organized mind. Besides—I hate crowds."

"But it's no fun if there aren't any crowds," she protested. "I like doing my Christmas shopping when everyone is hurrying around and Christmas carols are playing—"

"I don't." As far as he was concerned, that settled the matter. He expected her to put up more of an argument—she usually did—but she surprised him.

"Okay, Matt, whatever you say," she said meekly, slanting a look at him through her sooty eyelashes.

Matt's stomach tightened. When she looked at him with just that hint of a smile playing around her lips and with just that particular expression in her warm, dark eyes, he always wanted to pull her into his arms and kiss her thoroughly. And the way she had looked at him then, he'd known she knew exactly how he felt.

So far he'd managed to stick to his resolution not to let his desire for her overrule his common sense. He'd kept their kisses as casual as possible, although it had taken every ounce of willpower he possessed. He'd called on all his self-discipline to keep from touching her except in the most offhand, nonsexual way.

Paula. The more time he spent with her, the more he wanted her. He was sadly afraid that his plan had been a dismal failure. Not only was he not sick of her, he wanted to make love to her more than ever. Was she right? Should they give in to their mutual desire? She'd made it very clear that she would expect nothing from him—no promises of undying love, no diamond ring or proposal.

So what was stopping him? They were both consenting adults. Maybe if they made love enough times, their passion would die a natural death, and they could both get on with their lives and each find someone more suitable.

The more Matt thought about it, the more he liked the idea. But he wouldn't make a final decision yet. He'd wait and see what happened tomorrow. But tomorrow night, if he was still feeling the same way, and Paula gave him any kind of sign that she was, too, well . . . then . . .

Matt stared at the deep raspberry-colored rose sitting in the Waterford vase. Paula was very like that rose, he thought. Soft, sweet, fragrant. He grinned. Sultry, thorny, dangerous when you got too close.

What would it be like to make love with her?

Images raced through his mind. Paula in lacy underwear. Paula with her hair tumbling about her face. Paula with her lips swollen from his kisses and her body gleaming like fine porcelain in the firelight. Somehow he knew she wouldn't be a passive partner when she made love. She was probably just as enthusiastic about sex as she was about everything else.

He swallowed and tugged at his collar. Damn. It was warm in the office. His breathing quickened. He remembered touching Paula's breasts, how firm yet soft they'd felt in his hands.

He squirmed in his chair. Then he laughed softly.

That blasted woman! She was driving him crazy! No doubt about it. Something was going to have to be done about the situation. And soon.

Paula woke up Saturday morning with a feeling of breathless excitement. She'd been looking forward to this all week, ever since she'd realized she'd have Matt to herself the entire day. Although initially she'd been disappointed by his refusal to take her to Galveston, after a while the idea of helping him do his Christmas shopping was appealing. He was going to pick her up about nine o'clock—I like to get started early, he said—and they would shop and have lunch and shop again. If they were finished early they would see a movie—because we won't be hungry for dinner until later, he said—and then afterward they would go to dinner. Somewhere romantic, she hoped, because she had decided that today was going to be The Day.

She stretched languidly. Just thinking about Matt gave her a queer, mushy feeling in her stomach. The Day. This was The Day.

Tonight Matt Norman would forget all about his careful plans and do more than give her one of those chaste, completely sexless kisses. Tonight Matt Norman would lose his much-valued control. Tonight Matt Norman would make love to her.

She wondered what he'd be like as a lover. Remembering those early kisses, she had a feeling that once he let go he'd be a commanding, passionate partner. She shivered. It was delicious thinking about making love with him. Savoring it. Anticipating it.

After all, she'd been very patient. But she was through waiting. It was well past time for the knockout punch.

NINE

Paula wiped her mouth with her napkin, sighed, and sat back in her chair. "It's been a wonderful day, hasn't it?" She felt very mellow, thanks to two glasses of wine and a tender filet mignon. The muted sounds of conversation and clinking silverware surrounded them.

Matt smiled at her from across the table. "Yes. And I got most of my Christmas shopping done."

He looked quite pleased with himself. He also looked extremely handsome in the flickering candlelight. Paula loved to look at him. There was a lot to be said for dating an attractive man, she thought. She found she really enjoyed the envious glances she received from other women. Now, as they smiled at each other, she could feel a tingle of anticipation beginning again—the same anticipation she'd felt this morning. Soon they would leave the restaurant, and he would take her home. Her pulses quickened.

"Ready?" Matt asked. He drained his wineglass of the last few drops.

She nodded.

Outside it was a clear, still, starry night—one of

those rare evenings in Houston when the humidity was almost nonexistent. Paula took a deep breath and was seized with a rush of happiness. Throwing her hands in the air, she twirled around and around. "Oh, it's a glorious night!"

"Paula!" Matt said, glancing around the parking lot. "Someone might see you."

"So what?" She laughed, twirling faster until she felt dizzy and full of the sheer joy of being alive. "Come on, Matt," she urged. She tried to grab his hands, but he sidestepped, shaking his head. "Twirl with me . . ." Her words floated in the crisp air.

"Paula . . ."

"Come on. It's so much fun! Look, there's a shooting star!"

"You're nuts," he said. "We're in a public parking lot, for God's sake." He laughed self-consciously and tried to hold her still, but she slipped from his grasp.

"Who cares? Didn't you ever twirl with a partner when you were kids? We'd hold hands like this—" She grabbed his hands. "Then we'd lean back and twirl as fast as we could until we'd lose our balance and fall in the grass. Then we'd laugh until our sides hurt. Oh, it was wonderful!"

Now he was laughing, too, but he refused to budge.

"What a stick-in-the-mud you are!" she exclaimed. At this very moment, she was so happy she thought she'd burst. The only thing that she could think of that would make her happier was selling one of her songs. But since that hadn't happened yet, this—this feeling of delight and wonder—was enough to make her feel as if she were perched on top of the world, as if she knew something no one else knew, as if she'd be young forever.

Giddy from her jubilance as well as the twirling, she

staggered against Matt, and he clasped her upper arms to steady her.

"Whoa," he said, laughing in spite of his attempt to make her stop. "Steady now."

She threw her arms around his neck. "Kiss me, Matt. Kiss me!" She knew she was acting crazy, but she didn't care. Oh, life was good! Everything in her was singing, excited, full of anticipation and discovery. She wanted to capture this moment forever.

"Paula . . ." His voice sounded gruff.

She looked up. She could feel his heart beating against her own. "Kiss me," she whispered, tightening her arms. His hands slid from her upper arms to her back, and she closed her eyes.

His mouth was cool as he brushed a light kiss over her upturned mouth.

"No," she protested, weaving her hands into his hair, urging his head closer. "Kiss me as if you mean it."

For a long moment he stared at her, then his mouth captured hers in a long, drugging kiss—their breaths mingling, their mouths greedy, their tongues insistent. When he lifted his head, they were both breathless and shaken.

He released her slowly, his fingers caressing her cheekbone sending shivers down her spine. "Let's go," he said, his voice uneven and husky.

Yes, let's, she thought, the sound of her heartbeat like thunder in her ears. *Let's go to my house and light a fire in the fireplace and lie down on the floor and make love. Let's touch each other and kiss each other and fill ourselves with each other.* Just thinking about making love with him caused that melting, hollowed-out feeling deep in her belly, similar to the one she experienced when she stood in a high place and looked down. And that was exactly the way she felt, she thought. As if she were poised on a precipice and at any moment she'd fall, spinning into the unknown, into a place of dangerous delight.

As they drove to her townhouse she was acutely aware of Matt sitting only inches away. The inside of the car was dark and intimate. The lights of passing cars and the buildings lining both sides of the streets receded into the background. They held no reality for Paula. Only Matt, and the desire she could feel pulsing between them, seemed real.

She thought about how his mouth had felt, about its warmth and wetness and the faint taste of wine that lingered. She thought about how his tongue had felt when it touched hers, exploring and demanding. She thought about how his body had felt against hers—taut, strong, all male.

A tremor passed through her as she peeked at him. He was looking straight ahead. He hadn't said a word since they'd left the parking lot. She wondered what he was thinking and feeling. She wondered if he wanted her as much as she wanted him tonight.

One thing she knew for sure. No matter what he thought, Matt was not going to leave her at her door with a good-night kiss. Not tonight.

He still hadn't decided if they should make love tonight. He wanted to. His body was crying out for release. And he knew Paula wanted to. Desire had raged through them when they'd kissed. Why was he still uncertain?

Hadn't he already figured out that they would never tire of each other until they'd taken this step? If they were to sever their relationship without making love, each would always wonder about it, attaching more importance to it than actually existed. But if they succumbed to their desire, they would probably discover that there was nothing earthshaking about it. It was always the unknown that seemed the most desirable. Then they could part as friends with no regrets, and no questions in their minds.

When they arrived at her place, he'd go in with her and they'd sit down and they'd talk about it. That was very important, he thought. He always liked to have things clear and up front in any kind of relationship, business or personal. If everything was spelled out ahead of time, and everyone involved understood everything, there could be no misunderstandings or hurt feelings. Order in all things, that was a wise way to live.

Then, after they talked, they'd make love. He was already looking forward to it. Even if it wasn't earthshaking, Matt was sure the experience would be very, very pleasurable.

Savoring the tension building in him, he glanced at Paula. She had a dreamy expression on her face. He smiled. She was really something—half woman, half child. Imagine twirling around like a little kid in the middle of the Carillion parking lot on a Saturday night!

And you kissed her in the middle of the parking lot, don't forget that! God, it was a good thing their relationship was nearing its natural end, because if he spent much more time around her, he might find himself totally corrupted.

When they reached her place, it seemed to be understood between them that he would come in. She had left one light burning, a low-wattage hurricane lamp that graced her spinet piano.

"Matt, why don't you take off your jacket and make yourself comfortable?" she suggested. "Then if you like, you can build a fire in the fireplace. I'm going to go change clothes. I'm sick of these panty hose.'' She disappeared down the hall.

Before long Matt had a nice fire going, and he sat on one end of the couch and looked around. This was the first time he'd really had a chance to study Paula's place. Since they'd started dating, he'd purposely avoided being alone with her so he could stick to his resolve of keeping their relationship casual.

Although this room and what he could see of her dining area on the other side of the hall were more cluttered than the rooms in his house, he had to admit they were attractive, with a homey warmth that was appealing. Her furniture wasn't to his taste, but still . . . it seemed to fit her personality. She'd filled the room with a mixture of traditional and antique pieces, although the couch he was now sitting on was long, low, and more contemporary than anything else with its loose, plump pillows and inviting softness. And even though his preference in colors was grays and whites and pale mint-greens, and he'd have never paired a vivid aquamarine couch with navy-blue print wing-back chairs and a cinnamon-colored rug on the hardwood floor—he liked the overall effect she'd managed. Eclectic but inviting.

But the room needed order. There were too many things cluttering up the surfaces: porcelain and pewter cats, books, magazines, sheet music, candles in all sorts of containers and candle holders, red clay pots filled with well-tended plants, videos, records, tapes, an open notebook of staff paper that contained snatches of music, and a guitar propped in the corner.

And the walls. They were covered with framed Monet and Renoir prints, mixed with Currier & Ives watercolors, and family photographs, some of them old and yellowed. There was also an enormous poster of

Elvis Presley before he'd started to look ravaged and another smaller poster of the Beatles, as well as a beat-up framed poster of a young Ann Blyth sitting atop a grand piano and advertising *The Helen Morgan Story*. Matt grinned. He was an old movie buff; maybe he and Paula actually had something in common.

Wedged into another corner was the spinet piano, and on the floor next to it sat a basket filled to over-flowing with more music. Another basket tucked between the wing-back chairs held embroidery hoops and a jumble of colored threads and, on closer inspection, half-finished pieces of embroidery. Bemused, Matt shook his head. Was she interested in *everything*?

There were also small stuffed and rubber toys lying around on the floor. Matt frowned. Where *was* that cat? It made him nervous to sit there not knowing where she was. At any moment she could come out. The thought of her rubbing up against him nauseated him. He'd say one thing, though. Paula's house did not have a bad smell, as he had been inclined to believe all houses of cat owners did. In fact, her house smelled faintly of vanilla, a scent Matt had always favored.

"There. I feel much better now that I'm out of those tight clothes. Now what can I get you to drink?"

At the sound of her lilting voice, Matt glanced up. His heart nearly stopped. He knew he must be bug-eyed. He opened his mouth, but no sound came out.

What in God's name was she wearing? Was that a negligee? A red *satin* negligee? Heart pounding like a triphammer, Matt started to rise, but she glided over to the couch, stood in front of him, and gently pushed him back. Her lips were slightly open, and he could just see the very tip of her pink tongue. As she leaned over him, he got a good view of creamy breasts covered only by satin and lace.

"Now, Matt," she murmured. "You don't have to get up and help. I can take care of you."

Her words and voice were a silken promise, wrapping around him like a love song. Her skin smelled like sandalwood and incense and sweet spices. Lit from behind by the soft golden glow of the hurricane lamp, her hair swirled around her face with inviting softness, as if it were just waiting for his hands to delve into it. Her feet were bare, and her toes peeked out from under the hem of the negligee, their nails echoing the fiery color of the satin.

A little pulse throbbed in the hollow of her throat, and Matt had to restrain himself from reaching up, drawing her into his lap, and burying his face right there where his mouth and tongue could easily find that delicate beat. The red satin gown and robe embraced her body like a lover's caress—gliding, touching, teasing with sensuous ripples.

His hands trembled, and he swallowed convulsively. The only sounds in the room were the crackle and hiss of the fire and the slow tick of the clock above the mantel.

As if she could see the erotic images racing through his mind, as if she could feel the hot blood racing through his veins, as if she could hear his heart thudding up against his chest wall in a desperate attempt to escape, a slow smile curved her lips. The smile was pure temptress—sassy, knowing, seductive, and innocent.

She straightened, and every curve in her tempting body was clearly defined. She turned slowly, and looking over her shoulder with the smile in place, she walked slowly away, the red satin whispering over her pert fanny like a soft spring breeze.

Matt's mouth felt as if it were stuffed with cotton.

His hands were clammy; his pulse and heart were in a race to see which one could reach the finish line first. She glided toward the hurricane lamp. "I'll just switch this off first."

What the *hell* did she think she was doing?

"Paula," he said in a voice that sounded like a bullfrog's croak. "Uh, we have to talk."

"Of course," she said softly. Within moments, she was back with two brandy glasses in her hands. The amber liquid gleamed as she handed him one of the glasses. Wordlessly, he accepted it, automatically swirling the liquid, then burying his nose in the glass, as much to escape the sorcery of her smile as to savor the fragrance of the drink. He took a deep breath and willed himself to maintain his equilibrium. His control.

The brandy smelled like intoxication. It smelled like temptation. It smelled like trouble.

As much to gain time as anything else, he sipped, the fiery liquid sliding down his throat and into his gut. He looked up. His eyes met hers—those dark, endlessly deep, brown velvet siren-eyes that invited, teased, seduced.

Good God.

That's exactly what she was doing. This was a carefully planned seduction scene, right down to the provocative outfit and orchestrated movements.

Why, that little minx. It would serve her right if he drank his brandy as fast as he could, then left. This lady was dangerous. This lady wanted to call the shots. This lady planned to have her way with him.

The lady smiled again, her dimples echoing the invitation of her satin-clad body.

Jesus, Matt thought, *I feel like the fly must have felt when the silken web closed around him*. He didn't know whether to be angry or flattered or exasperated.

"Why don't we have some music?" she said.

Before he could answer, she turned on the stereo, inserted a tape, and soon the seductive strains of Spanish guitar filled the room.

In one fluid, graceful motion, she sank onto the couch next to him. One arm snaked around the back of the couch, not quite touching his shoulder. Placing her brandy glass carefully on the coffee table, she laid her head on his shoulder and rested her other hand on his chest.

"Goodness," she murmured. "Your heart is beating so fast. You must learn to relax, Matt. You're too uptight." And so saying, her hand crept up his chest, feathered over his neck, then stroked his cheek, coming to rest against the corner of his mouth, where it rubbed softly. "Now what was it you wanted to talk about?" she said.

"Paula," he said in a strangled whisper. "What are you doing?" He took her hand, intending to remove it from the vicinity of his ear, where it was now circling, causing a spiral of heat to ignite the nerve endings that hadn't been ignited by the first onslaught of sight and smell and touch generated by her. But the instant he touched her, she stiffened and cried out.

"What's wrong?" Alarm coursed through him.

"Oh! I have a cramp. Oh, Matt, it hurts!" she wailed, her face crumbling.

"Where?"

"Here, in my calf." Whimpering, she lifted her right leg, the negligee and nightgown falling away. Her slim, bare leg gleamed in the firelight.

Like a sleepwalker, Matt reached for her calf. Wrapping his hands around the silky skin, feeling the firm muscles beneath, he kneaded and massaged her leg, which she conveniently propped up on his lap.

"Oh," she moaned. "Oh, Matt, don't stop."

He knew he should. He knew if he had any sense at all, he'd turn her over his knee and give her a good spanking, which was just what she deserved for this . . . this crazy stunt. Didn't she know she could get in big trouble if she pulled this on the wrong person? What if he wasn't an honorable, decent person?

But he couldn't seem to stop. He was mesmerized by the feel of her warm, firm, scented skin, by the desire raging through him. Jesus, he wanted her.

He gave it one last try. "Don't you think we should discuss this before we—"

"Shh," she said, covering his mouth with her hand. "Don't talk. We've done too much talking."

His hands moved up, over her knee, and up again, until they were touching the softer skin of her thigh. She shuddered. He knew he was lost.

Soon she was lying back against the deep-cushioned couch, her leg draped over his body, and he was bending over her, one hand continuing its journey up her silken thigh, the other making a beeline for the place it had wanted to be ever since he'd laid eyes on her in that outrageous outfit—closing around one round, perfect, delectable breast.

She would make him lose control if it was the last thing she ever did. She would play him like she played her piano—slowly, seductively, until the keys did her bidding. She would woo him like she wooed her guitar—grazing gently over the strings, plucking and strumming until they melted under her touch. She would seduce him like she seduced her audience when she sang those old Helen Morgan torch songs—by combining her voice, her eyes, and the movements of her body as she made love to her listeners.

Knowing full well exactly what she was doing, she would touch him in all the places she knew would drive him mad. She would whisper to him, moan, sidle up next to him. She would turn on all the charm and sex appeal, use all the knowledge she possessed. And she wouldn't stop until he was jelly in her hands—until he lost that look of perfection, until he trembled and shuddered and did whatever she wanted him to do.

She'd show him that some things couldn't be analyzed. Some things couldn't be planned. She'd teach him a lesson, show him just how easy it was to turn all his carefully thought-out strategy into chaos, and in so doing, she would have the upper hand in their relationship.

And it was so ridiculously easy.

She smiled with satisfaction when she saw the expression in his eyes as he got his first good look at her in the red satin job Susan had given her in a fit of whimsy and that Paula had never worn until tonight.

She laughed to herself when he fell for the cramp routine and reached for her calf while she moaned and whimpered and urged him on. Poor guy. He tried to protest, but he was a goner and didn't even know it. She was savoring victory when he gave up all pretense of massaging the cramp and his hand slid slowly up her thigh in unmistakable surrender.

This is it, she thought. *I've won.* A surge of power filled her, and she knew exactly what she was doing as she tugged him down until she felt her back hit the cushions of the couch.

But her secret amusement teetered when he touched her breast, and it disappeared altogether as his mouth captured hers with heated possession and forceful demand. Her thoughts spun with dizzying speed, matching the tempo of her heart as his hands and mouth claimed her, branding her through the thin silk that covered her body.

Suddenly she was scared. This wasn't the way she'd pictured the seduction scene. She was supposed to remain cool and detached while he lost his cool.

She was supposed to stay in charge.

But he was definitely the one in charge.

His tongue tasted her lips. He nudged her over until she was lying on her side against the back of the couch, and he was lying next to her, holding her close as he kissed her face, his warm, moist mouth trailing over her eyelids, down her cheek, nestling in the hollow of her neck.

Her heart gathered speed; her breath came in shallow spurts as his hands moved over her body with agonizing slowness.

His hands. Oh, his hands.

Lightly, gently, as if they were worshipping her body, they studied, stroked, loved, teased. Over the tips of her breasts, stopping for a while to circle and arouse, then down, down, over her flat stomach, around to her bottom where their heat seared her as they tantalized, kneaded, molded. A liquid, molten pulse throbbed deep inside her as his hands continued their knowing assault.

Her skin was on fire.

She was on fire.

She moaned, deep in her throat, as his hands moved between them, nestling in the juncture between her thighs, finding her heat, finding the source of the fire that threatened to consume her.

"You smell so good; you feel so good," he said, his voice rough. His tongue licked at the hollow between her breasts as his fingers delved into warm flesh, circling, caressing. Paula's heart thrummed as she strained against him.

"Matt . . ."

Now it was his turn to say, "Shhh." He raised his head, took her mouth once more, tongue plunging deep and mimicking the movement of his fingers. All thought ceased. It no longer mattered who was the seducer, who was seduced. Suddenly Paula knew, with heart-stopping certainty, that what had started out to be a game was no longer a game. She also knew this was where she wanted to be, right here in Matt's arms, letting him do whatever he wanted to do with her or to her.

Happiness exploded inside just as his touch brought her to that precipice she'd imagined earlier. She arched against him. She was falling, falling.

"Trust me," he whispered. "Let it happen."

And she did. She stopped straining, stopped thinking, and just gave herself up to him. And the sensation was glorious—a shuddering, wonderful, free fall into pure pleasure. After her body had stopped trembling, he kissed her gently and smiled into her eyes.

"Help me get rid of these clothes," he whispered into her mouth, his warm breath filling her.

Shakily, she helped him. She was still trembling from the force of her response to him. But somehow they managed, and by the time they'd gotten down to his briefs, he was standing and lifting her up off the couch, holding her tight up against him, then stripping off the negligee, sliding his hands down her body as the silk whispered to the floor.

"You're so beautiful," he whispered as he looked deep into her eyes. His own eyes were golden and sparkling in the fire's glow. His hair was no longer perfect.

It tumbled over his forehead, and Paula reached one shaky hand up to touch it.

"You're beautiful, too."

He smiled, then he kissed her again—a soft, sweet, enticing kiss. He held her away from him so that no part of their bodies touched except the place his mouth had chosen as it trailed over her body. His tongue tasted her lips first, then with aching slowness, his mouth dropped down to her breasts.

Paula thought this must be heaven as pleasure spiraled through her. Her knees turned weak, and just when she knew she couldn't stand another tormenting minute of this exquisite pain, this sweet agony, he lifted the gown and pulled it slowly over her head.

Then he stood back and looked at her, a crooked smile curving his mouth. His eyes invited her. *My turn,* they seemed to say as they rested on hers.

Mesmerized, Paula reached out, touched his burnished skin, felt its heat and the tension masked beneath its smooth surface. Slowly, ever so slowly, she tangled her fingers in the crisp, curly hairs on his chest, trailing them over his nipples, smiling as he gasped.

Her hands slid over his body, his strong, smooth, athlete's body with its taut muscles, its limber grace, its beautiful symmetry. Joy sang in her veins, in the rush of her blood, as he moaned beneath her fingers. She could see his chest heaving as she slid her hands between the elastic waistband of his briefs and guided the briefs down, her breath catching only for a moment as she saw his full arousal. He clutched her shoulders as she touched him, crying out as her palm closed around him.

Now they were equal, nothing separating them but the sliver of air between them. They looked deeply into each other's eyes, and Paula held her breath. She wished she could capture this moment in its shimmering simplicity, its silent anticipation, its achingly sweet torment as her hand held him and her eyes held him and neither of them could look away. She felt his heat and the need coursing through him, just as it was coursing through her. A tremor passed over her body as his hands closed the distance between them.

He touched her, and her body answered him silently with its quivering expectancy. She felt consumed by it, and as his touch became more insistent, liquid warmth called to him, and she was once again on that precipice, looking down into a whirlpool of dark desire.

In one strong movement, he lifted her, then laid her gently on the couch. Swiftly, as their hearts raced and their bodies throbbed, he entered her with one bold stroke, thrusting deep, filling her and claiming her.

Her surrender was complete. It no longer mattered who was the victor or who was the vanquished. Her silly game of seduction no longer mattered. Nothing mattered except this man and this moment in time. She drew him in as far as she could, wrapped her arms and legs and heart around him, surrounding him as she was surrounded by him. Hearts thundering, bodies straining, wills meshing, they moved together. Neither closed their eyes. Instead they held each other's gaze, and Paula's only coherent thought was that she wished she could stay this way forever.

When he brought her to a shattering climax, lifting her before plunging her into the whirlpool, then lifting her again, she knew her life had been irrevocably changed.

She was so incredibly sweet. Once he'd gotten over the shock of her blatant seduction act, once he'd decided that this was exactly what he wanted, he had surprised himself by the feelings she'd evoked in him.

This was supposed to have been good, clean sex. Fun, but nothing earthshaking. Just two healthy people who wanted each other. No strings. No big deal.

Well, the joke was on him, wasn't it? It was the craziest thing, he thought as he smoothed her tangled curls and kissed the tip of her nose, but making love with Paula had just about brought him to his knees. Their lovemaking had been explosive, tender, agonizing, sweet, exciting, heated, wonderful, terrible, and earthshaking.

Now, curled up together on her couch, naked limbs entwined, sated in the afterglow of their lovemaking, Matt felt bemused, bewildered, bewitched. He grinned. He sounded like an old, corny love song.

"What're you smiling about?" she whispered, touching his mouth with the tip of her finger.

He drew the tip into his mouth and sucked on it gently. He stroked her shoulder, her arm. "I'm smiling because you've managed to tie me up in knots," he admitted. "I don't know whether I'm coming or going, and tonight hasn't helped."

"Good," she said, snuggling against him. "I like keeping my men off balance."

That was the trouble, Matt thought. If there was anything he hated, it was being off balance. He couldn't stand uncertainty or surprises. He didn't feel on top of things when he didn't know exactly what he'd do or say in any situation.

His relationship with women had all followed this pattern. He always set the pace. He was always the one who decided if, when, and how often they'd see each other. He was the one who took the lead in whether or not they made love. And they always discussed whether they would or not before they did. He had never allowed any woman to seduce him.

Until Paula.

Until tonight.

With his thumb, he traced the curve of her jaw, then touched her dimples, one by one.

"Nice dimples," he murmured, following his touch with a kiss.

Her arms tightened around him, and he let his palm rest against her breast. It felt wonderful beneath his hand, and the thought crossed his mind that he'd like to keep his hand there forever, caressing her warm, scented skin while his lips were pressed against her forehead and he breathed in the clean, fragrant smell of her hair.

He felt complete, happy.

Whoa, he thought. *Stop right there. Don't make more of this than it is. So it was sensational sex. So she's sexy and fun, and she makes you feel good. But don't forget she was entirely up front with you. She told you point-blank she's not interested in any kind of permanent commitment. She doesn't want marriage. And you do. So take it easy.*

But even as he told himself to be wary, he found himself stroking her breast, smiling as it peaked in his hand. And soon he was lost in the rhythm of their lovemaking—this time a slow, languid climb into pleasure that had them clutching each other and crying out with fierce abandon.

TEN

Paula had never been happier. She found herself day-dreaming constantly—just stopping in the middle of something and drifting off into dreams of Matt and their times together. She, the girl who abhorred all things traditional, had suddenly turned into a perfect cliché of a woman whose brain was so befuddled by her feelings for a man that she found herself actually looking at satin-and-lace wedding gowns and imagining herself in one.

"Oh, God," she moaned one day. "I have to stop this. What's wrong with me?" She had never dreamed she would fall so hard. For what else could it be? She loved the sex, true, but it was more than that, and Paula was too honest with herself not to admit it. She was panic-stricken by the thought, but it looked as if she'd been caught in her own trap. All her clever schemes to ensnare Matt had resulted in being ensnared herself.

But when she forgot about being scared, she sang a lot and danced a lot and smiled a lot. Half the time she floated through the days while she dreamed about the nights. Matt's face and eyes and smiles filled her thoughts and quickened her pulse. Reliving the love-making that had turned out to be something neither could seem to get enough of, she would feel her skin heating and her heart beating in slow, thudding rhythms.

She would be cleaning a pool, using the skimmer to scoop up dead leaves, and she'd suddenly stop. Just stop. And stare into space, oblivious of what was going on around her.

Erotic images raced in her brain. Matt's sun-splashed skin as he lay on his side sleeping in the early-morning stillness. The way his eyelashes looked against his skin when his eyes were closed. Matt's hands whispering over her body. Matt's mouth claiming hers.

She couldn't stop thinking about him. When she was with him, she couldn't keep from touching him. When she wasn't with him, she counted the minutes until she would be again.

People began to notice.

"Paula, you seem off in another world lately," her father said one day.

She sighed. "Yes, well . . ." Her voice trailed off.

"Want to talk about it?"

His eyes were gentle, his voice soft. Paula smiled. "Not yet, Dad."

He returned her smile. "I'm always available."

"I know."

A few days later, Paula, Kim, and Susan were having their biweekly dinner together. This particular night they had chosen Pappadeaux, a popular Cajun restaurant in the Galleria area. Although it was late November, the weather had turned warm again, and they were sitting in the courtyard sipping their drinks as they waited for their table. Lights twinkled overhead, and the quiet splash of the fountain mingled with the laughter of the other guests.

"Paula's in love," Kim announced.

"What?" Susan said, almost choking on her drink.

"I am not," Paula said, but even to her own ears she didn't sound convincing.

Kim continued as if Paula hadn't spoken, addressing her remark to Susan. "She's fallen hook, line, and sinker for one of the partners in the law firm where I work. A WASP. He wears three-piece suits. He drives a BMW. He's old-money Houston. His family lives in River Oaks. He's a *Republican*!"

"Paula?" Susan squeaked. "Our Paula? The same nonconformist Paula who wore a purple leather miniskirt topped by a purple lace see-through blouse to a sorority rush party once?"

"The very same," Kim said, blue eyes sparkling.

"They were stuck-up prigs," Paula said mildly. "They deserved it." But she grinned, remembering their shocked faces. It had been wonderful. She had loved making them all squirm as they tried to figure out how they could get rid of her without making a scene. "It was great, wasn't it?"

Kim and Susan both laughed.

"Can you see this guy standing on the sidelines while Paula marches for abortion rights or AIDS relief or gay pride?" Kim asked. "Can you see Paula walking down the aisle in a satin gown attended by thirty-three bridesmaids in rainbow colors?"

Eyes dancing, Susan said, "I thought you were the one who was never going to do anything so ordinary as fall in love and get married."

"You two are really asking for it," Paula said.

"Okay, forget the 'getting married' part," Susan

said. "Explain this 'falling in love' part. Why is it I haven't heard anything about this guy?"

Before Paula could answer, Kim said, "Let me tell her. I think I'm more objective about this situation than you are." Quickly, she related the events of the past month. "I told Paula her plan would backfire, and it has." Kim had a triumphant look on her face as she finished her story.

"So when do I get to meet him?" Susan said.

"Thursday."

"Thursday? Are you bringing him to your folks' house for Thanksgiving?"

Paula nodded.

"Oh, I can hardly wait," Susan said. "I have to admit, I never thought you'd fall for someone like this. I always thought I'd have to reconcile myself to having some long-haired artist or musician in the family." Then she laughed. "Actually, I never thought you'd get married. I thought you'd probably just live with some guy for twenty years and shake your poor mother's very foundations."

"Will you stop with the 'married' stuff? I'm not planning to marry the guy! We're just . . . just . . ."

"Yes?" Kim and Susan said in unison.

"Just lovers," Paula mumbled quickly. She could feel the blush creeping up her face, and she was furious with herself. The old Paula, the before Matt, rebel Paula, would have proudly declared she had a lover. "And he doesn't wear three-piece suits."

Kim hooted with laughter. "He might as well."

She was very glad that their names were called just then, because in the flurry of getting up and being taken to their table, the subject of Matt was forgotten, and Paula could relax.

She was a bit apprehensive about taking Matt to her

parents' house for Thanksgiving dinner, especially after Susan and Kim had teased her so unmercifully. On top of that, she wondered how poor Matt would fare. She'd warned him, though, telling him in great detail exactly what to expect.

He surprised her. He actually seemed to enjoy himself, and he was the perfect guest, charming her mother and impressing her father. Even her brothers acted as if they liked him. After dinner, Tony pulled her aside.

"Hey, Paula," he said. "I really like your new boyfriend. Try not to do anything to scare him off, okay?"

Paula gritted her teeth, biting back a retort. What good would it do? Tony was Tony. He'd never change.

Joey was sweet, though. "Matt's a nice guy," he said. "But he's a little conservative." Joey grinned. "You'll have to work on that."

She hugged him.

Joey's wife, Elaine, cornered her and whispered in her ear, "Is he as good in bed as he is to look at?"

"Elaine!" Paula said, feeling her face heat up.

Elaine laughed and winked. "I'm jealous," she said, but Paula knew she was only teasing. Elaine was crazy about Joey and made no bones about it.

When the afternoon was over, and Paula and Matt were both stuffed to the chin with turkey and dressing and all the trimmings, Paula's parents walked them to the door. Frank shook Matt's hand and said, "Hope we see you again, son."

Paula's mother smiled at Matt, her dark eyes eager. "The next time you come I want to hear how that case comes out."

Paula rolled her eyes. Talk about subtle. Her mother was about as subtle as a Mack truck. If her mother only knew that all her hopes were in vain, that Paula herself had squashed any chance of Matt ever thinking along the lines of marriage, she would die. A leaden feeling settled into Paula's stomach. She was the one who had said there would be no strings. She was the one who had said she wasn't interested in any permanent commitments. She was the one who had said she would expect no declaration of love. So she had no one but herself to blame if she got hurt. If she had any sense of self-preservation at all, she'd stop seeing him right now.

But she couldn't have stopped if she'd wanted to. And she knew it. All she had to do was see him or hear his voice, and she was like soft clay, ready to be molded into any shape Matt wanted.

They went everywhere together. Paula went to her first ballet, and Matt went to his first rock concert. She loved the ballet; she wasn't sure how he felt about the concert. She had to admit he was game, though. He actually wore jeans, but drew the line when it came to a T-shirt.

"I'll stick with a cotton shirt, how's that? Does that make you happy?" His voice turned husky as he caught her in his arms. "You know how much I like to make you happy."

Her heart leaped at the look in his eyes.

Matt took her to hear a zydeco band.

"I didn't know you liked this kind of music," she said.

"There are a lot of things you don't know about me," he whispered. He slipped his arm around her and his hand slid under her arm where it rested against the side of her breast.

For the rest of the evening Paula was acutely aware of his touch. She listened to the fast, seductive music, her body warm and waiting. When they finally left the dark, noisy club and walked out into the cool December night, Matt held fast to her hand and hurried her to his car. The door was barely shut when he reached for her.

"Oh, God, Paula," he said after the first wild, sweet kiss. "You're making me crazy. I can't think about anything else except you. Except this. I'm obsessed with you."

But she noticed he never used the word *love*. *Well, knucklehead*, she told herself. *What did you expect? You know better than anyone that Matt, like all men, is proud. He'll certainly never tell you he loves you unless he thinks it's reciprocated. Unless he thinks you might be changing your mind and your ideas.*

That night, after almost frenzied lovemaking, Paula sat in her darkened living room and thought about her dilemma. Matt had gone home because it was a weeknight and he had an important case going to trial the next day.

She had certainly gotten herself in a mess. She remembered that old saying, Be careful what you wish for because you might get it. Well, she'd wanted Matt as a lover, and now she had him. The trouble was unless she were willing to change, unless she were willing to become the kind of woman Matt wanted, she would not be able to keep him as a lover. Because Matt wanted a traditional life. The whole ball of wax: a big fancy wedding, a supportive wife, and children. If she married Matt she'd have to resign herself to living in a big house, doing charity work, entertaining Matt's friends and business associates, joining the proper clubs.

Could she do that? Did she want to? Because if she forged ahead, let Matt know she'd changed her mind, she had to be ready to accept the consequences. For once in her life, she couldn't just plunge.

Paula sat up most of the rest of the night. She cuddled Miss Milly in her lap and thought and thought. In two days, it would be Matt's birthday. The end of one year and the beginning of another. A rite of passage.

The clock on her mantel softly chimed the hour. Four o'clock in the morning. She yawned and stood. She'd finally made her decision. And deep down in her heart, she knew it was the right decision.

Matt was impatient for the day to be over. It was his thirty-fourth birthday, and he and Paula had reservations at Tony's. She had never been to Tony's, and he was looking forward to introducing her to the restaurant.

He felt a little guilty that he wasn't spending the evening with his parents, but his mother had been understanding.

"We'll have you over Sunday evening and celebrate your birthday then," she said, and Matt had agreed. Maybe he would even surprise his mother and bring Paula with him. He grinned as he thought of what Betty Norman's expression would be if he did something so completely out of character.

Paula had certainly changed him, he thought. Take the roses. She had finally admitted she was sending them, and now that they had stopped coming, he found himself missing them. She'd changed him in other ways, too. He no longer felt the world would come crashing down around him if he didn't finish every single thing on his checklist for the day. And he didn't work late every night, although Paula complained that he still worked far too many nights than was healthy.

Well, tonight he intended to quit early so he could go home and take his time getting ready for the evening. In fact, he intended to leave right now. Feeling like a kid playing hooky, he hurriedly stuffed some papers in his briefcase, then stopped. Why was he taking this work home? He wasn't going to work at home. He took the papers back out and stacked them neatly. Tomorrow was soon enough to deal with them.

He locked his desk, buttoned his jacket, turned out the lights, and walked out of his office. Rachel's startled eyes took in the briefcase.

"Are you leaving? Already?" She looked at the clock on her desk. It was four-fifteen.

"Yes. Good night, Rachel. See you in the morning." He whistled all the way to the elevator.

Within minutes he was unlocking his car and driving out of the garage. He tuned the radio to a rock station. Because Paula liked rock music so much, he was trying to learn to enjoy it.

He turned onto Louisiana, then turned again onto Prairie. He always took Memorial Drive home at night. He hated the sterile drive on the freeway, preferring the more picturesque scenery of Memorial Park and the winding roadway through the villages. There was really only one commercial area on his route, and that was close to downtown. But once free of that he could enjoy the view.

He slowed as he approached the traffic signal at the intersection of Westcott and Memorial, and suddenly his name leaped out at him from a billboard on the right side of the road. Astonished, he was past it before he'd had a chance to see if his eyes had been playing tricks on him.

Surely he'd imagined his name.

Surely that billboard he'd just passed didn't say MATT NORMAN in big red letters. He found a street to turn into so he could turn around, then he headed back the way he'd come, craning his neck to see the billboard.

Jesus. There it was.

He screeched to a stop, opened his car door and got out.

Across the street, high above the ground, was an enormous billboard. In huge red letters was the message:

HAPPY BIRTHDAY, MATT NORMAN
CAN THIS BE LOVE?
PAULA

His heart knocked against his chest as he stared at the words. What was she saying? That she thought she loved him? He couldn't believe it. Right out here in the middle of Memorial Drive, on a billboard as big as a football field, she was asking him if he loved her and hinting that she loved him.

What did this mean? Was she changing her mind about marriage and all the rest of it?

Lord, he was going to take an awful lot of ribbing about this. He could just hear Rory and the others in the office. And Benjamin Tobias! What would that old crank have to say if he got wind of this? His mind spun as he thought about his family, his friends, all the people who'd known him for years. What would they think?

But despite those worries, Matt was flattered. What man wouldn't be? After all, Paula was a beautiful, sexy, desirable woman, and she was declaring to the entire city that he was important to her.

As he slowly opened his car door, he knew he'd better think fast. In just a few hours he would be seeing Paula, and she would expect him to answer her question. Whatever his answer was, he'd better make damned sure he was certain how he felt. Because just as he'd always known, he'd have to live with the results of his actions. He was living with them right now.

Paula couldn't wait for the evening to be over. She was so edgy she felt like crying. From the minute she'd known she couldn't change her mind about the billboard, she'd been sorry she'd done it. But it was too late to take the words back now.

She eyed Matt over the rim of her wineglass. All evening, from the minute he picked her up until now, he'd been the consummate gentleman—attentive, sweet, gentle, and charming.

He smiled when she gave him the gift she'd picked out so carefully—a soft leather travel kit.

"It's perfect," he said. "Thank you." Then he took her hands in his and squeezed gently, his gaze meeting hers across the candlelit table.

He told her she looked beautiful. She'd worn a dress she knew he would especially like—a soft pink lace with a high neck and long sleeves. Ladylike and demure.

But he didn't say a word about the billboard. By the time their check came, Paula's insides were quaking. There could only be one reason he was being so sweet and kind and not mentioning the billboard until the evening was over. He didn't love her, and he was trying to let her down easy. He probably thought that was the gentlemanly thing to do—take her to Tony's, wine and dine her, and then explain to her that she just wasn't the kind of woman who would ever fit into his life. As a significant other *or* as a wife.

Her eyes filled with tears as he said, "Let's get you home. You look tired," then put her coat around her shoulders and guided her toward the door. Tired. She was sick at heart. She'd gambled, and she'd lost.

As they walked out into the cool night air, she

couldn't suppress a shiver, and Matt immediately drew her close and put his arm around her. But she wasn't fooled. He was just setting her up for the kill.

When they reached his car, he stopped, turning her to face him, holding her loosely in the circle of his arms.

"We haven't talked about the billboard," he said.

"I know." There was a knot in her stomach as well as a lump in her throat. Her heart knocked painfully against her rib cage.

"It was a crazy thing to do." He tipped her head up, and she could see his eyes glittering in the light from the streetlamp. "I've been thinking about your question," he whispered, "and I think I know the answer."

A frisson of fear raced through her, but she didn't lower her eyes. She'd never been a coward. She faced life head on.

"The answer is yes, I think this is love. What do you think?" Then he smiled, and Paula's heart did a handstand. Before she could answer, he lowered his head and kissed her half-open mouth sweetly, softly, touching his tongue to hers with infinite care in a loving, gentle caress.

Then he kissed her again, and she closed her eyes and wound her arms around his neck.

His words thundered in her brain. Yes, he thought this was love. *Oh, Matt, Matt.*

And then she stopped thinking entirely and gave herself up to his kiss, putting her whole heart and soul into her response, and it was a long time before they finally got into the car and headed for home.

The Houston media loved the billboard. It caught their fancy, and everyone was talking about it. One radio station devoted a whole evening to phone calls wherein the billboard was discussed. Paula had even been asked to appear on *Hello, Houston,* a local TV talk show.

Both daily newspapers did stories about the billboard. The *Chronicle* reporter interviewed Paula, but the *Post* reporter called the firm and asked for Matt.

When Rachel buzzed him to see if he wanted to talk to the reporter, at first Matt was going to refuse. But then he changed his mind. Maybe if he talked to the guy, he would have more control over what they printed.

The guy turned out to be a woman.

"Good morning, Mr. Norman," she said as she strode into the office. "My name's Marilyn Duffy. How does it feel to be an instant celebrity? And just exactly what did that question mean?"

When the interview was over, Rachel again buzzed him. "Mr. Claybourne said to tell you he'd like to take you to lunch."

A feeling of foreboding stole over Matt. When the head of the firm wanted to see you, it was usually something important.

"I'm worried about how Benjamin Tobias is going to react to this publicity you're receiving," Claybourne said when he and Matt were settled at their table. He eyed Matt, his pale-blue eyes somber. "You know how conservative he is."

"Well, there's not much I can do about it, so I guess we'll just have to wait and see," Matt said.

"Have you explained to this young woman of yours that we are a very dignified law firm, that you are up for a senior partnership, that hijinks like these might not be looked at very kindly?" Claybourne asked.

Matt met his gaze levelly. "No, sir, I haven't. Frankly, I simply don't see how what Paula did has any bearing on my work or my standing with the firm. It's a private matter."

"If our clients think we're lightweights, they might get nervous."

"My clients all know I'm not a lightweight," Matt countered.

"Look, Matt," Claybourne said more kindly. "I was young once, too, you know. But caution is the watchword here. I'm not suggesting that your senior partnership is in jeopardy. All I'm saying is it might be more advisable to keep a low profile."

Matt knew Oscar Claybourne wanted him to agree. But he wasn't about to let the older man off so easily. "Rory Sebastian has been involved in all kinds of stunts. No one has ever said a word to him. Why me?"

Claybourne sat silently for a moment. Then he said, "Rory Sebastian will never make senior partner. He's too flamboyant and too casual about his work. He doesn't have the skill or the intelligence you have, Matt. You're a brilliant young lawyer as well as the best litigator we have. Your future is assured. All you have to do is continue the way you've been going. Work hard, keep your nose clean, marry a nice girl, and take your rightful place in the community as well as the firm." He smiled. "That's my best advice."

Matt's jaw hardened. He felt like telling Oscar Claybourne to take his advice and stick it where the sun didn't shine.

"I know you're angry, Matt, but just think about what I said. That's all I'm asking."

And for days afterward, Matt could think of little else.

ELEVEN

Paula wasn't nervous at all. She'd thought she would be, because she'd never before appeared on television, but the hostess for *Hello, Houston,* Joni Jessup, a bouncy blonde with an infectious smile, put her at ease at once.

"Paula . . ." Joni began after she'd introduced her to the audience, "your billboard has captured the romantic imagination of the people in Houston. Why do you think that is?"

This was a question Paula was prepared for because she'd wondered about it herself. When she'd gotten the idea, she'd never expected anyone but Matt to care, and was astonished to find that thousands of people were talking about it and driving by to see it. In fact, one of the radio announcers said this morning that hundreds of people were stopping to take pictures of it. They'd caused traffic jams on Memorial, and now the police department had assigned an officer to direct traffic.

"I think it's because there's so little romance in our lives," Paula said. "All we ever read about is crime and war and homeless people and children starving. People are greedy for something that makes them feel good.''

''I hear that businesses along Memorial Drive are charging for people to park in their lots while they gawk and take pictures,'' Joni continued.

''Only in America,'' Paula said with a laugh.

''Paula, why don't you tell our audience about what prompted you to rent the billboard.''

So Paula happily launched into the story of how she and Matt had met, how she'd pursued him via letters and phone calls, how she'd taken dinner to his house, and even how she'd sent him one rose each day to remind him that she had no intention of going away. ''I figured men get away with this kind of campaign to woo a woman, so why couldn't I?'' She conveniently left out the part that she'd originally started her mission with the intention of getting Matt Norman to smile. It sounded much more romantic to let people believe it was love at first sight.

While she was telling the story, the audience laughed and applauded. Some of the women even cheered. Paula had a few guilty twinges as she thought about the fact that Matt might not like her revealing all this information about him on public television, but once she had started, she really couldn't quit. And the story *was* true. Surely he'd want her to be truthful.

''I was hoping you'd be able to persuade Mr. Norman to appear with you this morning,'' Joni said. ''We'd all like to meet him.''

''Well,'' Paula said, ''Matt's very tolerant of me and my whims, but he's a pretty private person, and he wouldn't have been comfortable up here talking in front of an audience.''

"A lot of men are uncomfortable talking about their feelings," Joni concurred. "Don't you agree?"

"Yes, I do. It's up to us women to try to change that. But it won't happen overnight."

"No, it won't," Joni agreed. "But we keep plugging away, don't we? Now, Paula, I'd like to talk about your music. In your bio it says you're a composer."

"Yes," Paula said proudly. "I haven't had much success yet, but my father always taught me that perseverance eventually pays off."

"And you're also a singer."

"I don't do much performing anymore. Now I'm concentrating on writing songs."

"Oh, but you promised me you'd do one of your songs for us. I hope you're still willing," Joni said.

The audience clapped, and Paula needed no more urging. Why, this was better than getting to sing the National Anthem at the Oilers game. "I brought my guitar along," she said with a grin.

She had chosen one of her newest songs—one of the ones she'd sent Lindy Perkins.

The lights on the set were dimmed, and a spot centered on Paula. She quickly tested the strings, adjusted two, then strummed a chord progression as an intro. "The name of this song is 'Lonely Lady,' " she said, then began to sing.

When you walked out of my life, you left an empty shell . . . what once felt like heaven, now feels like hell. Nothing's the same without you, and it never will be . . . nothing's the same without you, oh, please come back to me. This lonely lady needs you . . . your voice, your touch, your kiss. This lonely lady needs you . . . I can't go on like this.

Paula put everything she had into the song. She closed her eyes, thinking of Matt and how she'd feel if he were to disappear from her life as she launched into the second verse.

Even when I'm sleeping, my dreams are filled with you . . . and during the day you're always there no matter what I do. Nothing's the same without you, I need you desperately . . . nothing's the same without you, darling, please come back to me. This lonely lady needs you . . . your voice, your touch, your kiss. This lonely lady needs you . . . I can't go on like this.

When Paula finished, there was a hush, then a wild burst of applause and several whistles from the audience.

"That was wonderful, Paula!" Joni exclaimed.

Paula beamed, basking in the approval of her audience. Next to Matt and the way he made her feel when he kissed her or touched her or looked at her in a certain way, there was nothing quite as thrilling as applause. She felt a rush of adrenaline as she took her bows.

Matt and music. A perfect combination. As the applause died and the show wound to its close, Paula sighed. If only her career would take off like her love life.

She wondered if it might be possible to have it all.

Picking up the remote control, Matt switched off the television set. He had called Rachel earlier to tell her he wouldn't be in until noon. He knew she was surprised as well as curious. He could hear it in her voice, but he didn't explain.

He wondered how long it would take for Oscar Claybourne to hear about Paula's appearance on *Hello, Houston.*

Carrying his coffee with him, he opened the sliding glass door leading out to his walled-in courtyard. It was a sunny, clear December morning, with the temperature hovering in the mid-fifties. A plump robin was perched on top of the brick wall that faced the street. Matt's collection of windchimes sent soft notes ringing through the morning air. The begonias and impatiens he'd planted in the spring still bloomed in the sheltered flowerbeds and hanging baskets. Matt sighed contentedly.

From the moment Paula had started singing on the show, his emotions had been in turmoil. It was the first time he'd ever heard her sing. And it was the first time he'd had any idea whether she was any good—whether her songs were any good.

Matt was no expert on popular or country music, but he knew talent when he heard it. Before Paula had finished the first verse of her song, he knew it was good—that she was good. Damn good. Spellbound, he watched her, listened to her rich contralto voice as she sang the melancholy song. She was probably right, he thought. If she were to continue to work at her music as determinedly as she had worked at anything else she wanted—like him, he thought wryly—she'd probably be a star one day.

But the music business, from what Matt knew, was a tough one. It wasn't the kind of business a person could be successful at if it were just a hobby or sideline. It would be a demanding business, one that would have to come first.

Disquiet gripped him. Surely Paula realized that a life with him would preclude a career in the music business. Of course she must. Why, she hadn't even mentioned her music in weeks. There was no reason for concern. Still, she couldn't help but feel a bit cheated knowing she might be giving up the possibility of fame and fortune after working toward this goal for a long time. He would have to make it up to her, show her that she would always be a star in his eyes.

Matt finished his coffee and glanced at his watch. It was almost eleven. He'd better get going. But first he'd call Rachel.

"Oh, Mr. Norman," Rachel said, "I'm so glad you called. Mr. Tobias just phoned and said he was coming downtown to see you. I stalled him . . . said you were in court this morning, but he's going to be here at one o'clock." There was a worried edge to Rachel's voice as she continued. "I hope that was all right."

Matt grimaced. That was all he needed. Benjamin Tobias on top of Oscar Claybourne. "You did the right thing," he said. "Would you take care of something else for me? I'm going to leave the house in a few minutes, but I want you to call and order some flowers delivered for me—right away, okay?"

"Certainly."

"Good. Have the florist send two dozen roses to Paula Romano at this address—" he gave her the address of Frank Romano's pool-service company "—and on the card have them put: 'A star is born. Break out the champagne. We'll celebrate tonight. Love. Matt.' " Matt smiled, imagining Rachel's expression. "Got that?"

"Yes, I've got it." Rachel read the instructions back to him, and Matt's smile expanded. "Anything else?"

"Nope. See you in a little bit."

When Matt arrived at the office, it was quiet. The biggest majority of the employees of the firm took their lunch hour from twelve till one, and it was now twelve-thirty. Timed it right, Matt thought, glad he didn't have to field any questions about where he'd been all morning.

Rachel looked up from her book when he walked in. He waved a greeting. "Good book?"

"Yes." She turned it over for him to see the title. He grinned as he saw a long, glittering knife covered with blood. Rachel had a penchant for gory thrillers, and this was the way she usually spent her lunch hour—eating a sandwich and an apple while she devoured her paperbacks.

"Anybody miss me?" he asked, opening the door to his office.

"I covered for you," she said. "Oh, your mail's on your desk."

"Thanks."

By the time he'd leafed through his mail and checked his calendar, it was nearly one o'clock. At one o'clock exactly, his intercom buzzed.

"Mr. Tobias is here," said Rachel.

Matt stood, braced himself, then went out to greet his visitor. Tobias shook his hand, and Matt gestured him into his office. Tobias looked stern, and even though Matt told himself it didn't matter what the older man thought, he could feel his stomach muscles clenching. He hated disagreements and confrontations, and he was afraid that was exactly what was in store for him—not only now, with Tobias, but probably later, once Oscar Claybourne got wind of what had transpired on *Hello, Houston* this morning.

After Tobias was seated, Matt went around behind his desk and also sat. He waited, knowing he'd be at a disadvantage if he made the first move.

"Young friend of mine called me last night," Tobias said.

"Oh?" It wasn't what he'd expected Tobias to say.

"Told me to watch *Hello, Houston* this morning."

"Oh." Now he understood.

"Did you happen to see the show?"

Tobias's wintry gray eyes reminded Matt of cold steel. Matt met the older man's gaze straight on, without flinching. "Yes," he said quietly. "I did." He braced himself for the lecture he felt sure was coming.

Suddenly Tobias grinned, and it was like the sun had finally penetrated thick storm clouds. "She's really something, isn't she?"

Who was he talking about? Joni Jessup? At a loss, Matt simply nodded.

Tobias leaned forward and slapped the desk.

Matt jumped.

Tobias laughed. "You know, son, I had my doubts about you. Thought maybe you were a tight-ass like Claybourne and some others around here, and if there's anything I can't stand, it's a tight-ass. Man's got to be open-minded. Got to be willing to take chances. Got to be his own man—do what he believes in!"

"Oh, I agree," Matt murmured.

"But when I found out you were the man Paula's in love with, I knew there wasn't a thing to worry about as far as you're concerned, because any man Paula would pick would have to be my kind of man!" And so saying, Tobias stood and extended his hand across the desk.

Stunned, Matt stood, too. He grasped Tobias's hand.

"Surprised you, didn't I?" Tobias said.

"That's putting it mildly," Matt admitted. "I . . . uh . . . didn't know you and Paula knew each other."

"There's a lot you don't know about me, but from now on, we're goin' to get better acquainted," Tobias vowed. "Now sit down. We need to talk."

Later that afternoon Rachel came in and laid a memo on his desk. She had an odd expression on her face.

Matt picked up the memo and read it quickly. It was from Oscar Claybourne. It was short and to the point:

"Matt, please clear some time on your calendar for next week. We have some important matters to discuss and settle."

He'd initialed the bottom.

Well, Matt thought, whether Oscar Claybourne knows it or not, the matter of Paula is not open to discussion. She hadn't done anything wrong, and Matt didn't intend to let anyone insinuate that she had. But maybe he should talk to her. Not about the show or the billboard or anything like that, but about her plans. Surely she wasn't still entertaining the notion of a music career? She knew how he felt about marriage and children. She also knew exactly what he wanted in a wife.

Why, they'd talked about their views before they'd ever become lovers. She knew exactly where he stood and that he'd never agree to her continuing in the music business once they were married. Oh, she could write songs at home. He saw nothing wrong in that. But touring or performing or recording was out. She knew that. He was certain she'd worked things out in her own mind before she'd rented that billboard. And if there was any doubt in his mind, all he had to do was ask her.

But would it be fair to her to ask her to forget about a music career if he wasn't willing to make a permanent commitment to her first? Wouldn't she be within her rights to tell him to get lost if he tried to pin her down without declaring his intentions? But was he ready to ask Paula to marry him? Was he absolutely sure?

Shouldn't he wait, at least a couple of weeks, to be sure he really knew his own mind? In two weeks, it would be Christmas. Wouldn't that be a perfect time to ask Paula to marry him—if that was what he decided he really wanted?

Two weeks wasn't a very long time. Waiting would give both of them time to get used to the idea of going the next logical step in their relationship. After all, she was the one who would have to make a lot of changes in her life if they were to marry. But she would. There really wasn't any doubt in his mind that she would. Hadn't she already declared that she loved him—both on that billboard and on public television?

He smiled, remembering how sensational she'd looked and sounded on the program this morning. He could just see her singing lullabyes to their children. And when they gave dinner parties, she would sing and play the piano for their guests. She would be in great demand for charity shows and entertaining sick children at hospitals. She would be a credit to him and the firm. And if she sold a few songs, why, that might be nice. It wouldn't be stardom, of course, but it would make her happy.

He smiled. He wanted her to be happy. And he'd tell her she would always be a star in his book!

Paula was thrilled to get the roses. She read and reread the card. *A star is born*, he'd written. Her stomach fluttered with excitement. He was proud of her. He was coming to terms with her desire to have a music career! Why else would he have sent her this particular message?

Oh, everything was perfect. Matt's message only reinforced her opinion that he was changing rapidly. Why, she might get him in cowboy boots and a muscle shirt yet!

She daydreamed throughout the entire afternoon. Her

dreams were filled with images of herself being interviewed on *The Tonight Show*, with Matt sitting by her
side, smiling proudly. She saw herself at the Academy
Awards accepting her Oscar for Best Song from a
Movie and Matt beaming in the background. She pictured singers like Lindy Perkins and Whitney Houston
singing her songs. They would do a wonderful job.

But eventually fans of her music would want her to
record them herself. And finally, she would. She and
Matt would have homes all over the place, and the
walls would be covered with photos of her and famous
stars. They would divide their time between Houston—and where? Probably Alabama or Nashville. She
would tour, and they'd travel all over the world
together. He could be her manager as well as her legal
counsel.

She sighed, thinking about their life together and
what it would be like. It would be a perfect compromise. Matt wouldn't even mind giving up a full-time
law practice when he saw how important her career was
and how much money she could earn. And in return,
Paula would make a concession and have a big traditional wedding, which would not only satisfy the conservative side of Matt but would make her own mother
delirious with joy!

Finally the day was over, and Paula reluctantly put
away her hazy golden dreams. She could hardly wait
to see Matt.

She dressed for the evening carefully, wearing her
highest heels and her prettiest, most feminine dress. It
took much longer to dress than it usually did because
she had to field so many phone calls. It seemed everyone she knew wanted to congratulate her and comment
on her appearance on *Hello, Houston* this morning.

Even Mr. T. called, which surprised Paula so much she was speechless for once.

"Just wanted you to know I thought you were great this morning," he said.

"Oh, you *did* watch! I wasn't sure you would," she admitted.

"I wouldn't have missed it after you told me you were going to be on the show."

A warm feeling suffused her. "Thanks, Mr. T. That means a lot to me, coming from you." What a nice man he was.

"We're friends, aren't we?"

"Yes, and your friendship means a lot to me," she said.

"You plannin' to marry Matt Norman?"

The blunt question startled her. Then she laughed. "Well, he hasn't asked me, but I'm thinking about it."

"He'll ask you. He's too smart to let you go," Mr. T. said.

Paula frowned in bewilderment. "You sound as if you know Matt."

"Of course, I know him. He's my lawyer."

"Your lawyer! I had no idea."

"How could you? Don't recall we ever talked about my business affairs."

Paula smiled. "You're right, of course. Well, that's wonderful, Mr. T. I'm glad you approve of Matt, because he really *is* pretty special in my life."

After they hung up, Paula had to rush to be ready before Matt arrived. She just finished spritzing herself with Shalimar when she heard the doorbell, and she raced to open the door.

"Hi!"

"Hi!"

They grinned at each other. Then she was in his

arms, and he was kissing her, swinging her up off her feet, and holding her tight. She clung to him, closing her eyes and savoring the feel of him, the taste of him. When they finally broke apart and he set her feet back on the floor, she laughed up at him, still breathless from the kiss.

"You were wonderful today," he said, his green eyes sparkling like emeralds.

"I *was* pretty sensational, wasn't I?" She laughed again, feeling exactly the way she'd felt the night they'd first made love—full of the joy of being alive, full of excitement and the anticipation of all the new experiences she had to look forward to.

For the next two weeks she saw him almost every day. They did everything together, and it was the most exciting time of Paula's life. She'd never realized falling in love could be so fantastic. And Matt was wonderful. He was attentive and sweet and he did everything to please her. Paula was so touched by his efforts that she, in turn, tried to do all the things she knew would make him happy.

And he *was* happy. She could see the happiness reflected in his face and his eyes when he looked at her. She could feel it in his touch when they made love. She could hear it in his voice when he told her he loved her.

She was pretty sure he would ask her to marry him soon. She could hardly wait.

TWELVE

Paula could hear the phone ringing. "Oh, shoot," she said as she struggled to open her front door while juggling a bag of groceries. "I hope it's not Matt saying he has to work late again." It seemed like every time they made plans for an early dinner, something interfered.

Finally the door opened, and she burst through the doorway. Heart racing, she grabbed the receiver. "Hello?"

"Hello. Miss Romano?"

The voice was pleasantly low and female.

"Yes?" Paula fought to control her breathing. She would scream if this woman was selling something.

"Miss Romano, this is Kay Shelley, Lindy Perkins' secretary."

For a minute the words didn't register. Then suddenly, they did. Lindy Perkins' secretary! Paula's heart, which had begun to slow down from her mad dash to the phone, now speeded up once more, and her head whirled with dozens of disjointed thoughts. She gulped. "Uh, yes, Miss Shelley. Uh, hi." Good grief, she sounded like an idiot. What a stupid thing to say.

"Miss Perkins would like to speak to you, Miss Romano. Would you mind holding on just a minute, please?"

"Oh, s-sure, I'll hold on," Paula stammered. Her heart was pounding like a triphammer. *Oh, please, please, please,* she prayed silently. Miss Milly jumped up on the bar stool—her favorite spot when Paula was talking on the telephone—and began her loud purring. Paula absentmindedly stroked the cat while she waited, holding her breath and repeating her prayer over and over like a mantra.

"Hello? Paula? You don't mind me calling you Paula, do you?"

She would have recognized that smooth, rich-as-cheesecake voice anywhere. "Oh, no, Miss Perkins, not at all." Her stomach decided to play paddle ball with her heart.

A low chuckle. "Oh, please call me Lindy. None of this 'Miss Perkins' business. Agreed?"

"Oh, of course. I—" *Pull yourself together, nincompoop.* "I'd be honored to call you Lindy."

"I'm sorry it took me so long to listen to your tape, Paula, especially since I like it so much. If I'd had any idea what a gold mine I was sitting on, I never would have let it lie around such a long time."

She liked it so much! She called it a gold mine! Paula's heart once more skyrocketed into her throat, and her body felt like fireworks were being set off everywhere. "Oh, Miss Per . . . Lindy . . . that's wonderful." Her voice didn't sound like it belonged to her.

Another throaty laugh. "The boys and I are really excited about your stuff, and we were wondering if you'd like to come on over here to my place in Alabama for a few weeks to work with us. I'd like to

use one of your songs on the new album I'm puttin'
together.''

Paula gulped, almost speechless. "I . . . I'd be
thrilled. I . . . I can hardly believe this is happening!''

"Oh, it's happening all right," Lindy Perkins
answered, a teasing note in her voice. "You're a very
talented young lady, and I'm lookin' forward to workin'
with you. In fact, when you get here, if everything
goes well, and we hit it off, well, maybe we'll talk
about some other things I have in mind.''

Paula could hear the smile in the famous singer's
voice. She knew an idiotic smile was plastered across
her own face, too. In fact, her whole body felt like one
giant smile trying to burst out of her skin. She was
almost jumping up and down with excitement. Oh, she
could hardly wait to tell Matt and her father and mother
and brothers. Her brothers! Wouldn't they die? And
Susan and Kim. They'd be so happy for her. Oh, this
was the most thrilling thing that had ever happened to
her.

For the next ten minutes Paula and Lindy Perkins
talked about when Paula would come and what arrange-
ments needed to be made.

Finally, Lindy Perkins said, "well, that's it, then.
I'll have my secretary make your reservations for a
week from Saturday—that way you'll be home for
Christmas—and we'll plan on you stayin' about three
weeks. You sure you don't mind missin' New Year's
with your family?''

"No, of course not." What was New Year's compared to this?

"And there won't be any problem with your job?''

"No. None." This was the slow time of the year for
pool services, anyway, she thought. "Don't worry,
Miss Per—Lindy, I'll be there." Wild horses couldn't

keep her away. Nothing would keep her away. This was her chance at the brass ring, and she had no intention of missing it.

"Well, okay, then. Have a merry Christmas, and I'll see you soon. Oh . . . and, Paula?"

"Yes?"

"Thank you for sendin' me your music, honey. It's truly wonderful, and I can't wait to record it."

Paula's heart swelled. "Oh, Lindy, thank *you* for liking it so much. And Merry Christmas to you, too."

They said good-bye and hung up. Paula just stood there, in a trance, while thoughts tumbled through her mind in a joyful frenzy. Tears rolled down her face as her chaotic emotions eddied through her.

Miss Milly made a cooing noise, her way of talking to Paula, and Paula scooped the cat up in her arms, burying her face in Miss Milly's warm body. "Oh, Miss Milly, I'm so happy. I can't believe it! Lindy Perkins loves my music. I'm going to work with her and her band at her studio in Alabama! Isn't it wonderful? Isn't it fantastic?" Paula danced around the room while the cat struggled in her arms. Laughing and crying at the same time, Paula released the cat, then hugged herself.

"I don't believe it!" she shouted as she grabbed up the forgotten bag of groceries and dumped its contents on her kitchen counter. She picked up the package of frozen corn and the container of ice cream and thrust them into the freezer. Then she put the milk and plastic-wrapped package of strip steaks and the greens for salad in the refrigerator. The rest of the stuff got shoved into the pantry.

Still talking out loud, she started toward her bedroom. She was torn by a desire to call everyone she knew and shout out her news and the equally pressing obligation to hurry and take her shower before Matt showed up. She had invited him for dinner, and it was already six-thirty. He'd be there at seven-thirty, and she had a lot to do before then.

Just one phone call, she thought. She would just call Kim. She picked up the receiver, then put it down again. Matt deserved to be the first to know. As much as she wanted to share her fantastic news, she'd wait until she'd told him.

Still pinching herself, she headed for the shower.

Matt was filled with a pleasant tingle of anticipation as he rang Paula's doorbell. A month ago he had been sure that by now he would be sick of her. Exactly the opposite had happened. Instead of tiring of her, Paula had crept in and stolen his heart when he wasn't looking.

Incredible as it seemed, he was hooked. Paula was impetuous, unpredictable, impossible, and utterly irresistible. The more time he spent with her, the more time he wanted to spend with her. In fact, he could hardly stand to be away from her for one day. All the qualities that he'd thought would drive them apart had instead enriched his life. *She* had enriched his life.

He smiled to himself. Although it was a little frightening to admit it, he was seriously thinking in terms of a permanent commitment. Paula: she was the exact opposite of what he'd always thought he wanted in a woman, but now he couldn't imagine being with anyone else.

His life would never be the same, he thought, as the object of his musings opened the door, an eager smile lighting her face and eyes. She looked radiant in a candyapple red sweater and navy wool slacks. She pulled him inside and slipped her arms around him, lifting her face for a kiss.

"Hi," he said as he brushed her soft lips. "Um, you smell good." He allowed himself the luxury of burying his nose in her hair and holding her close for a long moment. God, she felt good, too, he thought as he hugged her against him.

He kissed her again, a longer, deeper kiss that had both of them breathing hard. When they finally broke apart, she said, "Whew. That was nice." Her eyes sparkled as bright as the lights on her Christmas tree. The thought crossed Matt's mind that he'd just as soon forget about dinner. He could think of something else he'd much rather be doing.

"I've got a lot more where that came from," he murmured, dipping his head to kiss her again.

Maybe something of what he was thinking shone in his eyes, because Paula laughed—that deep, sexy laugh that never failed to arouse him—and said, "Oh, no. No more of that now. I've got other plans for this evening." She pushed at his chest. "Let me go, Matt. There's time enough for that later."

Matt reluctantly released her, but he couldn't resist giving her saucy little bottom a pat as she walked away from him. She laughed again, then disappeared into the kitchen.

"Need any help?" he called.

"Nope. I've got everything under control. Fix yourself a drink. I'll have dinner on the table in just a few minutes."

Matt walked over to the bar where Paula had thoughtfully placed the ice bucket and a couple of glasses. He poured himself a generous portion of Scotch while he watched her on the other side of the bar. She was humming as she worked, and she looked up and grinned at him.

She certainly was happy tonight, he thought, as he walked back into her living room. She must have had a good day. Brushing cat hair off the sofa, he sat down. That damned cat of hers was still a bone of contention between them. The big calico gave him a wide berth; in fact, she usually hid behind Paula's dresser when Matt was there, but she left evidence of her presence everywhere. It drove Matt crazy to constantly have cat hairs all over his clothes. But Paula was adamant on the subject.

"Love me, love my cat," she'd say, a warning in her tone.

Matt fought the irritation he always felt each time he thought about that area of disagreement. They'd have to do something about a compromise if they did get married. He knew the matter of the cat would be one area where Paula would never give in. But it was too nice an evening to be irritated about anything. He felt good, and Paula obviously felt good, too. He was looking forward to a nice dinner and a romantic evening in front of the tree. Maybe they'd put Christmas carols on her stereo, build a fire in her fireplace—it was cool enough for one—and make love in front of it.

Matt closed his eyes, savoring the appealing images he'd conjured—he and Paula entwined, the flames leaping, the lights twinkling softly . . .

"Matt?"

He opened his eyes.

"Oh, good. For a minute I thought you were asleep."

He smiled. "No, just dreaming."

She smiled back. "Well, dinner's ready." Her eyes glowed with some inner stimulus.

What was it about her tonight? he wondered as he followed her into the small dining area where she'd taken great pains to set a really beautiful table, complete with lace cloth and candles. There was a bottle of wine cooling in a bucket of ice.

"I see you got the champagne," he said as he lifted the bottle. Good champagne, too, he thought. Tattinger's. He was impressed.

A secretive smile curved her lips. "I've had this champagne in the refrigerator more than two years. I was saving it for a special occasion."

Matt grinned. Of course. Hadn't he said they'd celebrate? Although he had a feeling there was something else going on, but obviously she wasn't quite ready to tell him what. Well, he'd indulge her—play along with her if it made her happy to keep him in suspense.

"Would you light the candles?" She handed him a pack of matches.

Matt obliged, and Paula retreated to the kitchen, returning with a platter containing two sizzling strip steaks in one hand and a bowl full of salad greens in the other.

"That looks good," Matt said. "I'm starving."

She served him a steak, and they both helped themselves to salad and French bread. Matt buttered his bread and took a bite, then cut a piece of steak, which soon followed the bread into his mouth. He chewed contentedly. "The steak is great."

"Thanks." She took a bite of her salad, giving him a sly look through her eyelashes. Matt could feel the energy in the air; she was full of suppressed excitement.

They ate silently for a few minutes, then Paula, who looked as if she might pop, laid down her fork and said, "I can't wait another minute." She handed Matt the chilled bottle of champagne. "This is going to be a day we'll remember forever." Her eyes glowed.

Smiling indulgently, Matt uncorked the bottle, and they both laughed when it frothed over the top. He filled both their glasses. Evidently Paula intended to make a production out of this.

Their gaze met once more as they raised their glasses, and Matt had a sudden intuition. He knew exactly what Paula was going to say. She was going to propose! The knowledge hit him with delightful certainty. He smiled as he watched her with tender, amused tolerance.

Would he ever get used to her? Or would she always do the unexpected? She couldn't stand to be traditional—to do things the way other people did them. He guessed he should be grateful she hadn't proposed via sky-writing, after what she'd done for his birthday.

"Oh, Matt," she said. "I'm so happy! I'm happier than I've ever been in my entire life!"

He knew he probably looked like a lovesick kid with that silly smile pasted on his face, but he couldn't help it. She might be outrageous, but he was flattered. And he *did* love her. She was unconventional, true, but at least their life together would never be dull.

He waited expectantly.

"This is the most exciting night of my life," she said, her voice bubbling.

His heart swelled with possessive pride. Tomorrow he would go to Tiffany's and pick out a ring. Wouldn't his parents be surprised?

"The most wonderful thing has happened to me, Matt, and I haven't told anyone else. I wanted you to be the first one to hear my news!"

News? What news? The rosy picture of Paula proudly showing off her engagement ring faded.

"Lindy Perkins called me today. She loves the songs I sent her! She wants me to join her and her band at her studio in Alabama and work with her on adapting one of them for her new album!" Paula's face split into a gleeful smile. "Isn't that fabulous?"

Matt felt as if he'd been punched in the stomach. A stillness settled over him as he listened to Paula gush on about Lindy Perkins and her phone call.

"And she said if things worked out well she had some other things she wanted to discuss with me. Oh, Matt, you don't know how long I've waited for something like this to happen, and even in my wildest imaginings, I *never* thought I'd get the chance to work with Lindy Perkins!" Her face was flushed, and she finished her champagne in one gulp, then laughed exuberantly. "Who knows where this might lead!"

Alabama. Recording studios. She was talking about leaving Houston. Leaving him. He stared at her.

"Matt?" She frowned. "What's wrong? You haven't said a word."

Stiffly, he forced himself to say, "Congratulations. I had no idea this was what you wanted." His hand tightened around the champagne glass. He looked at it as if he'd never seen it before, then raised it to his lips and drained the glass quickly. The wine burned all the way down.

She frowned, some of the excitement dying in her eyes. "What do you mean? You've always known I hoped to establish myself as a composer. In fact, I told you and your parents—that night we met them at Brennan's—about sending my material to Lindy."

"And you've hardly mentioned it since."

"That's not true. I—"

"You've talked about your job with your father more

than you've ever talked about music. I thought writing songs was just a hobby.''

"Matt, the reason I haven't talked about my music much is that people who aren't in the business don't really understand. They're usually bored by shop talk. Plus, I didn't want to jinx myself. I'm superstitious about things like that. But my music has always been the most important thing in my life. I thought you understood that.''

"How could I possibly think it was important to you? As far as I can tell, you haven't spent any time on it in the past six weeks. We've spent almost all our free time together. I don't know when you could have been writing songs.''

"Matt . . .'' Confusion flitted across her face. "Surely you realize that this past month or so has been a bit unusual?''

"I'm not sure I know what you mean.''

"I mean that the two of us were . . . We . . .'' A faint flush stained her cheeks, and she hesitated, licking her lips nervously. ''. . . we've been in that state of obsession that two people feel when they're falling in love,'' she said softly, ''. . . and the real world has sort of taken a backseat, but I always knew we'd have to come back down to earth one of these days.''

"I see.'' A coldness settled around his heart. He laid his fork down and pushed his plate away. He no longer felt hungry.

"Matt, please try to understand,'' she implored him. "I know we haven't had a chance to talk about our feelings for each other, but I'm sure you love me, and I know I love you. But I also love my music, and I always have. Don't ask me to give it up.''

"Oh, I understand, all right. In other words, even though you say you love me, I'm not important enough for you to put me first. Your music comes first, and I'll just have to take a backseat, like it or not."

"Matt, that's not fair!"

"Maybe not, but it's true."

"But, Matt, you even said a star is born in your note!"

"Yes, but I didn't mean it literally. I meant that in my eyes you were a star. I thought—"

"But music is my work. You, of all people, should understand that. Your work has interfered with our plans many times. Have I ever complained about that?"

"That's completely different, and you know it." How could she do this to them?

"How is it different?" Her voice sounded thick, as if she were going to cry.

"What you're referring to are minor inconveniences—me being late for a date or having to work a few hours on a weekend. What you're talking about doing will completely change our lives. You'll be in Alabama or Nashville or God knows where, and I'll be here in Houston. There's no comparison."

Paula heard the implacability in his voice, saw the rigidity of his body. She felt stunned, unable to grasp the shocking turn of events. She had never, not for one moment, imagined that Matt would be less than thrilled for her. In her naiveté, she had seen him grabbing her and swinging her around in the air while they both laughed and shouted. She had thought he would be as ecstatic and proud as she was. She had had visions of him calling his parents and bragging to all his friends and basking in her success. She had even entertained the hope that he would be able to take some time off and join her in Alabama for part of her stay.

Now all those rosy dreams were shattered as Paula stared at Matt's stony face and ice-cold eyes. Why couldn't he understand? Matt was so rational; his mind worked so logically. Why couldn't he see that he was being unreasonable?

His jaw set in an uncompromising line, he said flatly, "If you really love me, you'll forget all about this nonsense."

She swallowed. "That sounds like an ultimatum."

"It is. As far as I'm concerned, if you go to Alabama, you can forget about me. About us."

The stark words hovered in the air between them.

Her insides trembled as the realization hit her that he didn't want to understand, that he would never allow himself to understand. For if he did, if he was forced to see her side, he would no longer have control over his life. If he couldn't make her bend to his will, make her put him and his needs first, he would no longer know who he was. He hadn't changed at all. She'd just been kidding herself over the past weeks, thinking he'd loosened up so much, that he'd really accepted her for who she was.

She bowed her head. Tears burned behind her eyelids. Would it do any good to try one more time? She could feel him across the table—tensed, waiting for her decision.

Well, he had really given her no choice at all. She lifted her head. "Matt," she said quietly, "I do love you, but I cannot give up my dreams to prove it to you. I thought you'd accepted me for who I am, that you respected me, but I can see I was kidding myself. You want a woman who has no ambition or goals of her own—someone who will jump when you give the command. That's not me, Matt." She shook her head sadly. "That'll never be me."

He stood, face frozen except for a muscle that

twitched in his cheek, no emotion showing in his wintry eyes. "You're going to Alabama," he stated flatly.

"Yes."

Very carefully, he placed his napkin on the table. Then he pushed his chair back and turned away from her. Unable to move, she watched him walk into the living room, heard him pick up his coat, then walk to the door. Still frozen in place, she heard the door open.

For one heartstopping moment there was absolutely no sound in the house except the ticking of the clock and the sound of her own heart beating in her breast.

Then she heard the door close, the click of the latch as loud as a gunshot in the eerie stillness, and just as devastating.

THIRTEEN

The past eight days had been the worst eight days of Matt's life. They'd been miserable. Christmas without Paula. The weather, which had turned nasty and wet. But most of all—himself. With Paula gone, he couldn't drum up much enthusiasm about anything. His work, which ordinarily gave him so much pleasure and satisfaction, seemed meaningless. His home, always a source of delight and tranquility, seemed boring and dull. His goals, always so clear in his mind, now seemed murky and unappealing.

"Just what is your problem?" Rory asked on the Friday between Christmas and New Year's when Matt snapped at him. "Did I do something?"

"No, of course not." Matt was instantly sorry he'd taken his bad mood out on Rory. Inclining his head toward his office, he said, "Have you got a minute? I'd like to talk to you about something."

Rory's frown disappeared. "Sure."

That was one of the things Matt liked most about Rory—his ability to shrug off anything. He rarely held a grudge. Paula was like that, too, Matt mused.

198

"I need some advice," he said when he and Rory were seated.

"From me?" Rory grinned. "This is one for the record books. I can't remember you ever asking me for advice before."

"I've never had a problem like this before." Then Matt related the events leading up to his and Paula's argument.

"So you stormed out after issuing your ultimatum, and you haven't heard from her since." Rory's dark eyes were thoughtful.

Matt nodded.

"Have you tried calling her?"

"No." Even now, just talking about it, the same emotions churned through him. Anger, disappointment, a leaden feeling of betrayal . . . Why had she left him? If she really loved him, why had she gone? "Do you think I should have?"

"That depends on how badly you want to try to work something out with her."

Matt really hadn't expected any other answer. He knew no one could tell him what to do. That answer had to come from him.

"Do you love her?" Rory asked softly.

"I thought I did."

Rory raised his eyebrows. "Thought? You're not sure?"

"I'm not sure about anything anymore." Suddenly Matt could no longer sit still. He pushed his chair back, stood, then walked to the windows. Rain sluiced across the thick glass, and thunder rumbled in the distance. The skyline was almost obscured by thick, low-hanging clouds. A gray day to match his gray mood, he thought. Sighing wearily, he jammed his hands into his pockets.

"I've had my life all planned from the time I was

thirteen years old," he said slowly. "I've known exactly what I wanted, where I was going, and how I was going to get there. I've never wavered in my goals, and I've never had any doubts. Until now."

Lightning streaked across the charcoal sky, and the lights went out. Rory got up and joined Matt at the window. They stood silently for long moments, then Rory said, "Matt, we've been friends since we started kindergarten together at St. John's. We know each other's faults, and we know each other's strengths. I couldn't love you more if you were my own brother."

Matt's chest tightened. He felt the same way, but Rory had always been able to vocalize his feelings, something Matt found difficult. "Me, too," he finally said, then felt Rory's hand clasp his shoulder.

"So I'm going to give you the best advice I know how to give," Rory continued. "I think you should forget all about what you thought you wanted when you were thirteen and start fresh. If it makes you feel better to make a decision based on the pros and cons of the situation, then sit down and make two lists. On the first, list all the things that you don't like about your relationship with Paula. On the second, list all the things you *do* like. Then see which list is the most compelling. Ask yourself if you're better off *with* her than *without* her."

Another bolt of lightning zigzagged across the sky, and the lights flickered on, then off, then back on. In the sudden brightness, Matt blinked, then turned to look at Rory. "I thought you were going to tell me to forget my lists."

Rory grinned. "I wasn't finished with my advice. After you make those lists and study them carefully, wad them up and throw them away. Then do exactly what your heart is telling you to do right now."

Matt stared at his friend.

The grin faded from Rory's face, and he met Matt's gaze with unblinking solemnity. "Come on, old buddy. Be honest with yourself. You're crazy about Paula. I'd've had to be blind not to see how you feel. It was written all over your face when you were telling me what happened."

"But if she really loved me—"

"Bull!" Rory said. "Reverse that logic. If you really love *her* you won't let a little thing like pride stand in your way. Go after her, man. Take charge of your life. Grab that brass ring. It usually only comes around once."

Matt could hardly believe this was Rory talking—the same Rory who had had so many girlfriends he'd probably stopped keeping track of them. "I thought you were the guy who loved all women. Who couldn't ever settle for one because he'd be missing all those others he hadn't met yet . . ."

Rory's mouth twisted in a crooked smile. "Don't let this facade fool you. Under this Casanova exterior beats the heart of Romeo. I'm the biggest romantic on earth. I really believe in 'Some Enchanted Evening' and Cinderella and all those fairy tales. I just haven't met the right woman yet. I thought you knew that."

"So you're saying I'm a fool."

The smile grew bigger. "No. I'm saying I think you should start learning everything you can about entertainment law!" Then he winked, and squeezed Matt's shoulder again. "Well, I gotta go. Got a hot date tonight." He went off whistling.

Lindy Perkins looked younger in person than she did on television and in the movies, Paula decided. And she was funnier, too. Lindy had a dry, I-don't-take-myself-too-seriously kind of wit that Paula found refreshing.

It was New Year's Eve, and Paula had been in Alabama for five days—five busy days where she and Lindy and a few of the members of Lindy's band had spent long hours going over "Lonely Lady" and two other songs of Paula's. The whole process of selection and refining fascinated Paula, and working with the musicians—seeing the way their contributions and suggestions would mold and shape the final product—was an invaluable learning experience. But underlying all the excitement was a thread of sadness Paula simply couldn't banish. What should have been the most thrilling time of her life, perched on the cusp of success and the fruition of all her dreams, had turned out to be a bittersweet victory.

She missed Matt. There were dozens of things she wanted to share with him, and her fingers itched to pick up the telephone and call him. During the day he was never far from her thoughts, and during the night, images of him filled her dreams. The plain and simple truth was that she loved him and was slowly coming to the realization that nothing would ever be as good without him.

But Matt had made his position perfectly clear. She would have to be willing to give up her own ambitions if she hoped to share his life. And Paula knew she could never do that. As much as she loved him and wanted him, she could never be that old-fashioned, stay-at-home wife he seemed to need so badly. Of course, the past week she'd also come to realize that Matt would have never been content to follow her around the country, either. Neither of them had had a very realistic view of the other, which really wasn't surprising now that she thought about it. They'd spent very little time actually communicating. They were too busy trying to combat their almost overpowering physical attraction that they'd forgotten to be honest with each other.

And now they were suffering. Well, Paula amended, *she* was certainly miserable. She couldn't speak for Matt.

Today was New Year's Eve, and Lindy had given the "boys," as she referred to the members of her band, a couple of days off.

"They deserve some time with their families," she explained to Paula. "Hope you don't mind, hon."

"I have nothing to rush home for," Paula said, swallowing against the lump in her throat.

So the two women had puttered around the house most of the day. Lindy's husband Clint, a very quiet and unobtrusive man, had taken their two German shepherds into town with him—to keep him company while he ran errands. Now Paula and Lindy were sitting out by the glistening kidney-shaped pool, shaded from the bright sunlight by a large pink umbrella. The January weather was mild with a clear blue cloudless sky. It was such a beautiful day, Paula thought. She should be ecstatically happy. Instead she felt like crying. She sighed heavily.

"That's at least the tenth time I've heard you sigh this afternoon," Lindy Perkins said, her soft voice holding a touch of amusement. "Must be somethin' really heavy to make you so unhappy."

Paula wasn't sure what it was—Lindy's kind heart or her own need to unburden herself, but she soon found herself telling the famous singer all about Matt. She told her everything, including the way Matt had acted about the opportunity presented by Lindy and the trip to Alabama.

"I just think he was being incredibly selfish," she finished. "Don't you?"

Lindy smiled. She took a long swallow of her glass of iced tea, then said slowly, "Honey, when you've been around as long as I have, you'll realize that things are never that black and white."

"You don't think it was unreasonable of him to think I would give up this chance when it's everything I've hoped for and dreamed of for years?"

"Most men like to feel they're the most important thing in your life," Lindy answered. "Perhaps that's not so unreasonable. Shoot, I'm the same way. I need to know that in Clint's eyes, nothing is more important than me. There's no doubt in my mind that Clint always puts me first."

"You think I was wrong? You think I should have stayed in Houston? Thrown away this opportunity?" Paula knew she sounded incredulous. She had fully expected Lindy to agree with her.

"I don't think it's a case of right and wrong," Lindy said thoughtfully. "I was just tryin' to make you see that it really doesn't matter if you were right or your friend was right. What matters is that he sees this as a threat to your relationship, and if you care for him, you have to understand that and try to make him feel secure enough so he won't feel compelled to issue ultimatums."

Paula didn't answer for a long moment. It was very quiet in the secluded yard. Only the softly circulating water in the pool and the whine of a jet overhead broke the silence. "So you think I should have made an effort to contact him before I left."

"All I know is that I have ten gold records and three platinum ones, but none of those records will keep me warm at night and none of them will be fittin' companions for my old age.'' Then the singer smiled. '' 'Course, I'm a bit older'n you, too. Maybe I see things differently.''

''Yes, but your husband obviously supports your career.''

Lindy smiled. ''Clint is my second husband,'' she said softly. ''My first one didn't last long. I had a lot of years to be alone before I realized I'd have to do some compromisin' if I hoped to keep a relationship from fallin' apart.''

Paula wondered what compromising Lindy was talking about. It appeared to Paula that Clint was the one doing all the compromising.

''Clint and I have an agreement,'' Lindy said. ''From March through August we live in our home near Knoxville where Clint tends to our horses and ranch and gets everything in order. Then from September through February we divide our time between the road and our home here where I've got the recording studio.''

''And this works?''

''Yes. It works because we stick to it even if we occasionally change the rules. It works because we're willing to work at it.'' She smiled again. ''It works because we love each other very much and we don't want to lose what we have.''

Hours later as she lay wide awake in her room, Paula thought about Lindy's advice.

Should she have tried harder with Matt? Should she have swallowed her pride and called him? Maybe he was having second thoughts but was too proud or pigheaded to call her. Would it have killed her to make some attempt to patch things up? Maybe Lindy was right, and Paula and Matt could work out something acceptable to both of them. Maybe he'd just stalked off in anger, before he'd really had time to think things through. Maybe he'd be willing to compromise as Lindy had suggested.

Suddenly Paula desperately wanted to talk to him. To say she was sorry they'd fought, sorry they'd hurt each other. And what better time than tonight? It was New Year's Eve after all—the start of a new year—a perfect time for new beginnings.

She picked up the phone. It was only nine o'clock in Houston. She dialed the familiar numbers and waited, heart beating faster as she fought against a sudden nervousness. What if he were cold, what if he acted as if he didn't want to talk to her? *Cross that bridge when you come to it*, she told herself, then chuckled. She sounded just like her mother.

But she needn't have worried about his reaction. The phone rang and rang on the other end. She let it ring twenty times, then finally hung up. He wasn't home.

Well, what had she expected? It was New Year's Eve. He'd gone to a party or something. Paula grimaced. What a fool she was. He was out, more than likely with some other woman. Some tall, slinky, sultry other woman. Someone who looked like the blonde— Jill—who had been at his house that first night when Paula had taken the Chinese food over.

Maybe it was just as well. She was on the verge of an exciting career, one that knew no limits. Did she really want to be tied down to someone like Matt— someone who would make so many demands on her that she'd be lucky to be able to find any time at all to devote to her career? And with that question circling in her mind, she tried to tell herself she would get over Matt, that she was probably better off without him.

For the hundredth time that evening, Matt wished he hadn't come. A person should spend New Year's Eve with someone he loved, or spend it alone, he thought morosely. But Rory had insisted, so here he was, wishing he were anywhere else.

"Honestly, Matt," Sarah said, "you could at least *try* to act as if you're having a good time."

Matt jumped guiltily. Sarah's blue eyes studied him, amusement flickering in their depths.

"I'm sorry, Sarah. I don't know what's the matter with me lately. I'm not much fun to be around."

"Oh, it's okay. Don't worry about it." She grinned. "Come on, let's dance. It's New Year's Eve—time to make merry." She took his hand, pulling him out to the middle of the room, which Rory had converted to a makeshift dance floor. "It's a nice party, isn't it?" she asked.

"Yes," Matt agreed. Too bad he was in no mood to enjoy it. Too bad he was in no mood to enjoy anything these days. As he pulled Sarah into his arms and they moved together to the slow beat of the music, he clenched his jaw. It had been ten days since he'd stalked out of Paula's house, ten days since he'd seen her, and he was no closer to putting the episode behind him than he was that night.

Someone gripped his shoulder. He stopped, and he and Sarah moved apart.

"Matt, there's a telephone call for you," Rory said.

Matt frowned. Who would be calling him here? No one even knew he was coming here.

"It's your mother," Rory said. "You can take it in my bedroom. It's quieter in there."

What in God's name did his mother want? More annoyed than anything else, Matt entered Rory's bedroom, shut the door behind him, and picked up the receiver.

"Mother?" He heard a click and knew Rory had hung up the other phone.

"Matt? Oh, Matt, thank God I've found you."

His mother's voice sounded odd, and suddenly Matt knew a sense of foreboding. "What is it, Mother?"

"It's your father, he—"

Alarm streaked through him. "Dad! Has something happened to Dad?"

"Oh, Matt." She choked back a sob. Now he knew why her voice sounded so strange. It was thick with tears. "I'm so afraid. Your father's had a heart attack. He . . . he wasn't feeling well when he came home from work this afternoon, and—"

"Tell me the details later," Matt said, heart thudding in his chest. "Where are you?"

"At University Hospital. They've put him in intensive care. I'm using the phone right outside the unit."

"I'll be right there."

Rory wouldn't let Matt go alone. He insisted on accompanying him, and Matt didn't have the strength to argue with him. Even Sarah wanted to come, but Matt drew the line at that. He didn't want to have to worry about Sarah on top of everything else. All he wanted was to get down to the hospital and see for himself what was going on. He was more afraid than he'd ever been in his life. And what scared him more than anything was the fact that his mother, who always seemed so perfectly in control of her emotions, so detached and amused about everything, had been so frightened.

When he and Rory walked off the elevator Matt's mother was waiting. Her eyes were swollen and red, her face haggard, and for the first time in his life Matt realized his mother was getting older, too. Tonight, with no makeup and dressed as she was in black slacks and a plain gray sweater, she looked every bit of her sixty years. Her hands trembled when he took them and leaned down to kiss her. Tears welled in her eyes as they drew apart.

"Oh, Matt, I can't lose him," she said.

Matt's own eyes misted. He felt totally impotent.

"Come on, Mrs. Norman . . . Matt," Rory said. "Let's all go sit down over there."

After the three of them were seated in the waiting area outside Intensive Care, Matt's mother told them what had happened.

"I had just taken my shower," she began in a shaky voice. "Your father had been lying down, and I shook his shoulder to tell him it was time for him to start getting ready." She twisted a handkerchief in her hands, then sniffed and dabbed at her eyes. "He . . . he seemed so tired, and I even said maybe we should stay home." She turned imploring eyes to Matt. "I thought he was coming down with a cold. The weather's been so awful."

Matt took her hand. It felt cold. He'd never seen his mother so distraught. In fact, he couldn't ever remember having seen his mother cry before. "It's okay, it's okay," he said, patting her hand awkwardly. His mother had always been so strong. But now she seemed frail and bewildered.

She shook her head, the tears spilling out and down her cheeks. Her bottom lip trembled. "It's not okay. Nothing will ever be okay again if Matthew dies." She began to cry, her thin shoulders shaking. "Oh, God, I can't lose him. Not yet."

Matt folded her into his arms, a lump forming in his throat. He wanted to cry, too. His gaze met Rory's over his mother's shoulders. Rory looked as stricken as he felt.

Finally his mother seemed to regain some measure of control, and she blew her nose and tried to finish her story. "Anyway, your father wouldn't listen. He insisted he felt fine. He said he knew I'd been looking forward to the party for weeks." Her eyes reminded Matt of the storm clouds that had blanketed the city for days. "I didn't give a damn about that party!"

"Of course, you didn't, Mrs. Norman," Rory soothed, and Matt shot him a grateful look.

"I . . . I helped him get up, and he seemed dizzy, but he got mad when I said again that I thought we should stay home. *'Quit coddling me, Betty,'* he said. 'I'm fine.' " She bit her lip, and Matt was afraid she was going to start crying again, but she took a ragged breath, then went on.

"He went into the bathroom to have his shower, and I started blow-drying my hair." She swallowed, and she clasped her hands tightly together in her lap. "I heard the shower start. Then a few minutes later, I thought I heard a funny thump, but the blow dryer makes so much noise that I didn't really pay any attention to it." Tears filled her eyes again. "Oh, God. I'll never forgive myself if he dies. If only I'd shut that damn blow dryer off sooner!"

"Mother, quit blaming yourself. Please tell me the rest," Matt begged.

"When I finally finished with my hair, I started laying out my clothes, and I realized your father had been in the shower an awfully long time. You know what a quick shower he always takes."

Matt did know. His father had reproved him many times over the years because Matt, like most teenage boys, would commandeer the shower for thirty or forty minutes and think nothing of it. Both his father and his mother had lectured him about wasting water and monopolizing the bathroom and any number of other things.

"I can take a shower in five minutes," his father had been fond of saying. Matt smiled now, remembering, thinking how much he'd like to hear his father lecture him again. About anything.

"Anyway," his mother continued, "I began to get an odd feeling. Like something was wrong. I . . . I opened the bathroom door and called your father's name. He . . . he didn't answer. Finally . . . oh, God, my heart was pounding so hard I could hardly breathe, I pulled back the curtain and he was lying there on the bottom of the tub." She shut her eyes, her face white, and Matt was afraid she was going to faint.

"Hang on, Mother," he said, putting his arms around her once more.

Her whole body shook. "Oh, Matt," she said, her voice muffled against his sport coat. "I called 911 and I tried to revive him myself and the paramedics came and they said he'd had a heart attack and they . . . they brought us both here . . . and it was terrible. I was so scared."

Once more Matt's and Rory's gazes met. Matt knew the same worry he saw in Rory's dark eyes was reflected in his own.

Paula decided she was a glutton for punishment. She called Matt's house at two o'clock in the morning, again at four o'clock in the morning, and again at six o'clock in the morning.

There was never any answer.

The only conclusion she could draw was that Matt had wasted no time in finding another woman whose bed he was now warming. Where else would a man be on New Year's Eve?

Well, he could be at an all-night party, a little voice inside her said.

Oh, sure, Matt just loves parties, another part of her chided. He's the original party animal.

She finally fell asleep about seven on New Year's Day. She woke at noon with a raging headache and a sore throat. She felt like someone was pounding on the top of her head with a hammer and jabbing at her throat with needles.

I want to go home. I want my own bed, my own house, and my very own fat, cuddly cat. I also want Matt. Oh, God, she wanted Matt. She had to try to make things right between them.

When she walked out into Lindy's bright kitchen, Lindy took one look at her and said, "Uh oh. Bad night?"

Paula nodded. "Lindy, would it be all right with you if I call the airlines and see if I can get on a flight home today or tomorrow instead of staying until the middle of the month?"

"Honey, if you have to go, you go . . ."

"I've got to get my personal life straightened out before I can concentrate on my music. You understand, don't you?"

Lindy nodded, her beautiful amber eyes soft and knowing. "Sugar, I understand perfectly. You call me after you find out how that man of yours feels about things, and we'll work somethin' out. Somethin' that'll keep everybody happy—you, me, your guy, and—" She grinned, reaching for Clint's hand. He looked up from his bacon and eggs and smiled at her. "—my guy," she finished.

Paula hugged her. She hoped she'd be just like Lindy someday.

Then she hurried over to the telephone to call the

airline. They told her if she could be at the airport for the two o'clock flight to Atlanta, they could have her in Houston tonight.

"Oh, that's great," she said.

Later that day, as Lindy and Clint stood next to her in the terminal at the small Huntsville airport, Paula thanked them both.

"Shoot, sugar, we loved havin' you. Why, Clint and me, we don't have any kids of our own, and you're just the kind of daughter I wish I did have," Lindy said. Her blond hair blew across her face, and she swiped it back. Her smile lit up her face.

"That's right," Clint drawled. "You can come stay with us anytime. That goes for your fella, too."

Then Lindy hugged her, and Paula returned the hug warmly.

"Good luck, sugar. Let me know how everything turns out."

"I will," Paula promised. And as she turned to answer her boarding call, she wondered what she'd find when she got to Houston. Would Matt want her now? Would he be willing to find a way to work things out between them? Or was it too late for them?

FOURTEEN

Matt's father regained consciousness at five o'clock the next morning, nearly thirty-four hours after suffering the heart attack.

"You can go in for ten minutes, no longer," the doctor told his mother. He turned to Matt. "Then you can see him for five minutes."

When his mother came back out into the waiting area, she gave Matt a tremulous smile.

"How is he?" Matt asked.

"He's going to make it. I'm sure of it," she said.

Matt felt a tightening in his chest as he walked into his father's room. He looked so small, as if he'd shrunk, and there were so many wires. Good Lord, they had him hooked up to so many machines. "Dad?" he said softly.

His father turned toward him. His green eyes glittered in the semidarkness. "Hello, Matt." His voice sounded raspy.

"Don't try to talk," Matt warned. "Save your strength."

"Matt, I have to tell you something. If . . . if I don't make it—"

"Don't talk like that. Of course you'll make it."

"—please watch out for your mother."

"Dad," Matt said. "You know I will. Now take it easy. Don't talk anymore."

But his father seemed determined to go on. "She's not strong like you think, Matt. She depends on me. We're a team."

Matt knew that now. He'd seen the evidence of it through the past twenty-four hours. "I know," he said quietly.

"She's the best thing that ever happened to me," his father said. Then he smiled. "Your Paula reminds me of her."

When Paula finally arrived in Houston it was ten o'clock at night, blustery and wet and cold. She shivered as she clambered into the Park 'n Ride shuttle. As they bounced along to the remote parking lot, Paula wondered how Matt would react when she appeared unannounced on his doorstep.

She hadn't called her parents or Kim to tell them she was returning to Houston. When she left Alabama she decided to go straight to Matt's house and if he wasn't there to wait until he returned. She wanted to know where she stood, and she had no intention of going anywhere until she did.

The house was dark when she pulled up in front. But she really hadn't expected anything else. It was almost eleven. Ringing the doorbell and knocking on the door elicited no response.

Where was he? Had he gone somewhere? Or was he just out for the evening again? She walked around to the garage and stood on tiptoe to peer through the windows. Although it was dark, she could just make out the shape of the Fiat. The BMW was gone.

He was out. But tomorrow was a workday. Matt never stayed out this late when he had to go to work the next morning. He would be home at any moment. What should she do? she thought wearily. She was so tired. And so disappointed. She'd gotten herself all geared up for seeing him. She just wasn't sure she could stand going another night without knowing how he felt about her. Whether there was a chance for them.

She trudged down the walk, oblivious to the rain that still fell steadily. Hugging her raincoat around her, she opened her car and climbed in. Then she curled up on the seat to wait and closed her eyes.

It was seven o'clock in the morning before Matt could leave the hospital. By that time he'd gone almost fifty hours without sleep, and his mother was worried about him driving home.

"I'll be all right," he insisted.

"Get some sleep," she said. "Dad's out of the woods now, so there's no reason for you to hurry back here."

She looked rested, he thought. "Okay," he agreed. "But I'll be back tonight so you can go home."

"Elizabeth will be here tomorrow," his mother said. "She'll help out, too."

All the way home Matt thought about what he'd learned in the past few days. He thought about his mother and his father and their relationship. He thought about what his father had told him. But he mostly thought about Paula.

As he drove down his street, he was very glad to see his house. He was so tired, and everything ached. He couldn't wait to shave and take a shower. Then he planned to climb into his bed and sleep for at least six hours. Maybe after that he'd feel human again.

He found his garage-door opener in the glove compartment and pressed it. But just as he was ready to swing into his driveway, he saw the red Toyota parked out front. He frowned. PJR, the license plate read. Why, that was Paula's car!

His heart slammed into his chest, and he hit the brakes. Was something wrong? What was Paula's car doing parked in front of his house?

He yanked open his door and got out. Almost afraid to look, he walked over to her car and peered inside. There was a lump on the front seat.

The lump moved. Matt stared in astonishment as dark curls emerged followed by two sleepy brown eyes.

He looked as if he'd been through a war, Paula thought as she came fully awake. He looked as if he hadn't slept in days. His eyes were red-rimmed, and there was at least a two-day growth of beard on his face. His white shirt was badly wrinkled, and his pants—well, they simply didn't look like any pants the meticulous Matt Norman would ever wear.

She sat up, opened the door, and got out.

"Paula, what are you doing here?" he asked.

Her heart sank. He certainly didn't look happy to see her. "Waiting for you," she said.

"But—"

"I came last night, but you weren't here. I intended to sit in the car and wait until you got home. I . . . I guess I fell asleep." No smile. No warmth in his eyes. He stared at her as if she were a ghost.

"I've been at the hospital for the past two days," he said woodenly.

Alarm jolted Paula. "What's wrong? What happened?"

Matt sighed. His shoulders slumped, and Paula's heart constricted. She wanted to reach out and touch his hair, but she still wasn't sure if she should. Right now she didn't know if he'd want her to stay or order her to go. Maybe he hated her for walking out on him. Maybe he never wanted to see her again. Maybe she had no right to touch him or offer comfort.

"It's my father," he said. "Uh, look . . . do you want to go inside? I'm so tired I can hardly stand up."

"Oh, of course. Maybe I could make you some coffee." Something had happened to his father. And she hadn't been here. *Oh, Matt, I'm so sorry I let you down.*

The house smelled musty and damp. Once they were inside, Matt sank into a kitchen chair and haltingly he told her what had happened.

"Oh, Matt. I'm so glad he's going to be okay." Then she reached out and did what she'd been aching to do. She smoothed his hair back. "I know how much you love him."

He raised his eyes. "Paula—"

"Matt—" Her heart zinged at the look in his eyes. Was it going to be all right after all?

"I'm sorry," he whispered. "Can you ever forgive me?"

"I'm the one who's sorry," she said. "Can you ever forgive me for leaving you?"

Her hand trembled as he grasped it and held it against his neck. She could feel the bristles of his beard and the warm pulse beating under his skin. Oh, she loved him. Success would mean nothing without him.

"I was wrong. I know that now. I should never have asked you to give up your dreams. So many things are clear to me now. Things I never understood before."

"I was wrong, too," she said. "I didn't even try to understand how you were feeling."

"We should have talked more."

Happiness flooded her, and she grinned. "We were too busy making love."

But he didn't grin back. Instead he stood and pulled her into his arms. "Paula, I love you. We can work out our differences if we're both willing to compromise."

"I know that, Matt. That's what I came home to tell you!"

He finally smiled, and the smile made her stomach go all funny inside, like it was melting. "Does that mean you'll marry me?" he asked.

"I don't suppose you'd consider living together in sin?" she teased.

"Absolutely not. I want the world to know you're mine!"

"Well, what choice do I have then? I guess I'll have to marry you!"

His hands loosened their tight grip, sliding down her arms, then pulling her close. His mouth nuzzled the corner of hers, and Paula's heart leaped at the tender touch. "Tell me you love me," he said, framing her face with his hands.

"Of course I love you. Why else would I come home two weeks ahead of schedule and sit outside all night long waiting for you?"

"Oh, Paula, I've learned so much the past week, the past few days. All my careful plans—all my ideas—nothing meant anything without you to share them with."

"I know. I discovered the same thing. Without you, my life simply isn't complete."

"We're going to be so happy together," Matt said. "I'll sell this house—"

"Oh, no you won't. I love this house!" she declared. "We'll live here until we have our first baby. We'll turn the study into my office, and I'll write music there while you're at work all day.''

"I was planning to learn all about entertainment law and travel around with you," Matt said. "Of course, I was hoping you'd want to have a couple of kids someday. Preferably a boy and a girl that look exactly like you with brown eyes and brown hair."

"I want six kids. All blonds like you." She grinned.

He grinned back, but then her heart knocked against her chest as his eyes darkened with desire. They fastened on her mouth and he said, "If we're going to have six kids, don't you think we'd better get started immediately?"

"I thought you'd never ask," Paula said, already pulling her coat off and her sweater over her head and tossing it to the floor.

And then he was kissing her and Paula knew it really didn't matter where they lived or who gave in on what point. All that mattered was that they would be together. Two hearts meshed into one.

SHARE THE FUN . . .
SHARE YOUR NEW-FOUND TREASURE!!

You don't want to let your new books out of your sight? That's okay. Your friends can get their own. Order below.

No. 17 OPENING ACT by Ann Patrick
Big city playwright meets small town sheriff and life heats up.

No. 18 RAINBOW WISHES by Jacqueline Case
Mason is looking for more from life. Evie may be his pot of gold!

No. 19 SUNDAY DRIVER by Valerie Kane
Carrie breaks through all Cam's defenses and shows him how to love.

No. 20 CHEATED HEARTS by Karen Lawton Barrett
T.C. and Lucas find their way back into each other's hearts.

No. 21 THAT JAMES BOY by Lois Faye Dyer
Jesse believes in love at first sight. Now he has to convince Sarah of this.

No. 22 NEVER LET GO by Laura Phillips
Ryan has a big dilemma and Kelly is the answer to *all* his prayers.

No. 23 A PERFECT MATCH by Susan Combs
Ross can keep Emily safe but can he save himself from Emily?

No. 24 REMEMBER MY LOVE by Pamela Macaluso
Will Max ever remember the special love he and Deanna shared?

No. 25 LOVE WITH INTEREST by Darcy Rice
Stephanie & Elliot find $47,000,000 *plus* interest—true love!

No. 26 NEVER A BRIDE by Leanne Banks
The last thing Cassie wanted was a relationship. Joshua had other ideas.

No. 27 GOLDILOCKS by Judy Christenberry
David and Susan join forces and get tangled in their own web.

No. 28 SEASON OF THE HEART by Ann Hammond
Can Lane and Maggie's newfound feelings stand the test of time?

No. 29 FOSTER LOVE by Janis Reams Hudson
Morgan comes home to claim his children but Sarah claims his heart.

No. 30 REMEMBER THE NIGHT by Sally Falcon
Joanna throws caution to the wind. Is Nathan fantasy or reality?

No. 31 WINGS OF LOVE by Linda Windsor
Mac & Kelly soar to heights of ecstasy. Will they have a smooth landing?

No. 32 SWEET LAND OF LIBERTY by Ellen Kelly
Brock has a secret and Liberty's freedom could be in serious jeopardy!

No. 33 A TOUCH OF LOVE by Patricia Hagan
Kelly seeks peace and quiet and finds paradise in Mike's arms.

No. 34 NO EASY TASK by Chloe Summers
Hunter is wary when Doone delivers a package that will change his life.

No. 35 DIAMOND ON ICE by Lacey Dancer
Diana could melt even the coldest of hearts. Jason hasn't a chance.

No. 36 DADDY'S GIRL by Janice Kaiser
Slade wants more than Andrea is willing to give. Who wins?

No. 37 ROSES by Caitlin Randall
K.C. and Brett join forces to find who is stealing Brett's designs. But who will help them both when they find their hearts are stolen too?

No. 38 HEARTS COLLIDE by Ann Patrick
Matthew knew he was in trouble when he crashed into Paula's car but he never dreamed it would be this much trouble!

No. 39 QUINN'S INHERITANCE by Judi Lind
Quinn and Gabe find they are to share in a fortune. What they find is that they share much, much more—and it's priceless!

No. 40 CATCH A RISING STAR by Laura Phillips
Fame and fortune are great but Justin finds they are not enough. Beth, a red-haired, green-eyed bundle of independence is his greatest treasure.

Kismet Romances
Dept. 491, P. O. Box 41820, Philadelphia, PA 19101-9828

Please send the books I've indicated below. Check or money order only—no cash, stamps or C.O.D.s (PA residents, add 6% sales tax). I am enclosing $2.75 plus 75¢ handling fee for *each* book ordered.
Total Amount Enclosed: $_____.

___ No. 17	___ No. 23	___ No. 29	___ No. 35
___ No. 18	___ No. 24	___ No. 30	___ No. 36
___ No. 19	___ No. 25	___ No. 31	___ No. 37
___ No. 20	___ No. 26	___ No. 32	___ No. 38
___ No. 21	___ No. 27	___ No. 33	___ No. 39
___ No. 22	___ No. 28	___ No. 34	___ No. 40

Please Print:
Name _____
Address _____ Apt. No. _____
City/State _____ Zip _____

Allow four to six weeks for delivery. Quantities limited.